MICHAEL KEATON ANDY GARCIA

DESPERATE MEASURES

MANDALAY ENTERTAINMENT PRESENTS "DESPERATE MEASURES" PRODUCED BY BARBET SCHROEDER SUSAN HOFFMAN GARY FOSTER LEE RICH STORY BY DAVID KLASS DIRECTED BY BARBET SCHROEDER

mandalay ENTERTAINMENT

www.sony.com

DISTRIBUTED THROUGH SONY PICTURES RELEASING
IN CANADA: DISTRIBUTED THROUGH COLUMBIA-TRISTAR FILMS OF CANADA

desperate MEASURES

A novel by Robert Tine

Based on the screenplay
written by David Klass

BOULEVARD BOOKS, NEW YORK

DESPERATE MEASURES

A Boulevard Book / published by arrangement with Mandalay Entertainment

PRINTING HISTORY
Boulevard edition / August 1997

The Putnam Berkley World Wide Web site address is
http://www.berkley.com

ISBN: 1-57297-349-8

BOULEVARD
Boulevard Books are published by The Berkley Publishing Group,
200 Madison Avenue, New York, New York 10016,
a member of Penguin Putnam Inc.
BOULEVARD and its logo are trademarks
belonging to Berkley Publishing Corporation.

PRINTED IN THE UNITED STATES OF AMERICA

10 9 8 7 6 5 4 3 2

desperate
MEASURES

prologue

They didn't come along all that often but *this* was one of those stories that the news directors of television stations just loved to get their hooks into—one of those stories that had just about everything, a story tailor-made for television news. All the elements were there: a brave, smart, and, most important of all, *photogenic* child, facing death from a disease—a disease rare enough to be remote to the viewers of the five o'clock news, but familiar enough to put that little fear in your mind, that element of self-identification: *What would I do if this happened to* my *kid?* . . .

On top of that the kid, Matt Connor, was the son of a San Francisco cop—an important one—an inspector, no less—and, twisting the knife a little deeper, Matt had lost his mother in a tragic car accident some years earlier. The best part, though, was that there *might* be a happy ending—though that wasn't guaranteed. Matt could be saved, cured of his disease, but he needed a bone marrow transplant and so far a matching donor had not been found. So, to find out if plucky little Matt made it, then you had to keep watching.

Time was running out. . . . Would brave little nine-year-old Matt Connor beat the odds? Stay tuned.

But though the succession of pitiful circumstances may have been perfect fare for a television news director, they were deadly serious for Inspector Frank Connor, SFPD, and the WPIX reporter, Dawn Yoshioka, who had been assigned to the case.

The young television news reporter knew that she was supposed to be a dispassionate observer and reporter, but the cause of Matt Connor had drawn her in more than she expected it would and she featured it four times in a week, the news director of her station objecting not a bit to the extensive coverage, giving her as much of the news budget as she required. It was a story that had entered the collective consciousness of the San Francisco Bay Area; the predicament of little Matt Connor was discussed around water coolers, on talk radio, and in columns of the *San Francisco Chronicle* and the *News*; the Connor story had the other television stations in the market playing a desperate game of catch-up.

Matt Connor had seen his father on television and had heard his own plight described so many times that he scarcely noticed it anymore. The television set was switched on in Matt's room at San Francisco Memorial Hospital, tuned to the news, but he only glanced at it. Dawn Yoshioka and his father appeared on the screen, leading the news, the story following immediately after the headlines that opened the broadcast.

Matt was sitting up in his hospital bed, working on a balsa wood kit, a detailed model of a World War I biplane, a 1916 Spad XIII American, the workhorse of the famous Lafayette Squadron. He worked slowly and carefully, assembling the delicate struts that supported the upper wing of the fragile little craft, holding his breath as he put each piece in place. He was only half listening to Dawn Yoshioka describe his own life-or-death plight.

". . . As most of you know by now the man beside me is Inspector Frank Connor of the San Francisco Police Department. . . ."

Frank Connor looked tired and haggard, worn out by the trial he faced with his son. "My son, Matthew, is nine years old," he said, blinking into the strong lights in front of the television camera. "He has something called acute myelogenous leukemia . . ."

Matt glued the tiny struts in place with precise drops of adhesive, each bead the size of a seed pearl. Many boys Matt's age liked airplanes, but Matt was obsessed with them, fascinated by any kind of flying machine, from the crude wire-and-canvas aircraft of the First World War, up to complex spacecraft that were still nothing more than diagrams on NASA drawing boards.

". . . Matt desperately needs a bone marrow transplant," Frank Connor continued. "But so far we haven't found anyone who has DNA compatible enough for him to accept a transplant from them. . . ."

DNA . . . somehow those three letters had become the acronym of the waning years of the century. It seemed that there was hardly a story these days that didn't touch on DNA in some way.

The camera pulled back a little, to show Dawn and Frank standing side by side, Dawn holding the microphone and looking at Frank as he spoke. Her concern for the man and his son radiated off the screen.

"We have been through the available genetic registries," Frank said, continuing. "And thanks to Dawn and WPIX this is our third public appeal. The trouble is, most people haven't been tested, so there may be a donor out there somewhere, we just can't find him." Then he added: "Or her."

Frank Connor's voice seemed to grow taut in his throat, then broke slightly. He paused for a moment, overcome by emotion. In anyone else it might have been done for effect—but that was not Frank Connor's way. It was the silence that made Matt look at the screen.

Frank looked down and viewers could see that he was struggling to regain his composure. But the moment passed in an instant and Frank Connor began to speak again, his voice weak at first, but quickly gaining in strength. His eyes blazed with passion.

"The test takes only a couple of minutes," he said, looking straight into the camera lens. "And it doesn't hurt—you feel nothing more than a pinprick. Really. All the major Bay Area hospitals will perform the test free of charge. . . ."

The moment of strength in Connor's voice had drained away. It was replaced by a rising note of desperation. "So *please* get yourself tested. Matt is running out of time. You may have the power to save his life hidden within you. And you might not even know it." Frank Connor raised his hands open palmed, as if begging for a miracle.

An 800 number flashed at the bottom of the screen, as Dawn Yoshioka took over. "We are showing numbers to call where you can—"

Matt picked up the remote, pointed it at the television set, and clicked it off. He settled in his bed for a moment, then turned back to his model, working on it, absorbed by it, burying his fear in his concentration.

chapter 1

Four hours north of San Francisco, almost on the California-Oregon border, is redwood country. The landscape is a picturesque blend of the tall stately trees, the peaks of the Coast Ranges, and the rugged Pacific coastline. It is an odd setting for a prison, but one is up there—the Pelican Bay Correctional Facility—and it might be the toughest, most secure penitentiary in the United States, possibly in the world. It was home to Peter McCabe.

The fact that the donor was in Pelican Bay gave Frank Connor a moment's pause—but only a moment. His son was so sick that he would not have cared if McCabe had been a resident of hell. The problem was, getting to someone in such a high security prison would not be easy.

Once Frank Connor had pulled off the illegal miracle of finding a donor match on the FEDIT computer, he had pulled all the strings he could to get an interview with McCabe, a task made easier by the cooperation of Connor's immediate superior, Jeremiah Cassidy.

Both men had lied, telling the California State Board of Corrections nothing about the real reason they wanted to interview McCabe—they would deal with that later—saying, vaguely, that they thought the prisoner would be able to clear up some old, open cases they had been carrying for years now.

Once permission to see McCabe was granted, Connor lost no time getting up to Pelican Bay to see him. Cassidy went along, claiming that he might be able to speed things along, but he was anxious to keep an eye on his subordinate as well. Matt's illness had pushed Frank to the very edge, and Cassidy was secretly afraid of the lengths to which Connor might go to get a donor for his son. It was bad enough that Connor and Nate Oliver had broken into a secure federal database—one that was supposed to be off-limits to law enforcement agencies below the federal level—and he was afraid that Connor's next step might be even more drastic.

But even Frank Connor was sobered by the long criminal record of Peter McCabe. As they drove north, Frank at the wheel, Jeremiah clipped through the thick folder, giving the highlights of Peter McCabe's long and grisly criminal career.

"This guy is the real thing," said Cassidy, flipping through the pages of the file as if perusing a catalogue of crime. "Aggravated assault at twelve years old, which earns him two years in Youth Authority. . . . He's out at fourteen, back in at fifteen."

Frank Connor took his eyes off the road for a moment to glance over at his chief. ''What did he do that time?'' he asked.

''Manslaughter,'' said Jeremiah Cassidy, his voice matter-of-fact. It was hard to get that hardened cop facade to slip. ''And that was way back—before manslaughter became fashionable with the teen set.''

''Then what?'' Connor asked.

''He gets out at eighteen but he goes back in just two years later.''

''What for?''

''Double homicide,'' Cassidy replied. He was silent for a moment as he read the file a little more closely. The crimes were violent and were committed at an early age, but more interesting was the psychological profile that went along with the rap sheet.

''Listen to this. McCabe has no formal education beyond the fifth grade, but he's been tested and his IQ is over 150. He has been classified as having a sociopathic personality type. He exhibits no remorse whatsoever for any of his crimes. Not even when he was a kid.''

''You find no remorse unusual?'' Connor asked. ''I can't remember the last time I busted anyone who gave a shit about it or what they had done.''

Cassidy nodded. ''No, maybe not. . . . But how many of them had genius IQs?''

Frank Connor shot his chief a half smile. ''There's the difference: I don't think I've ever arrested an evil genius. Evil, yes, *definitely*. Genius . . . I don't think so.''

Jeremiah Cassidy had read countless criminal profiles during his fifteen years in the San Francisco

Police Department, but there was something particularly fascinating about Peter McCabe's file.

McCabe had been getting press since his first conviction and a number of clips were included in his file. First there was a Xerox of an old article from the *San Francisco Chronicle* headlined "Fifteen-Year-Old Convicted of Manslaughter." A picture accompanying the article showed a teenage Peter McCabe looking straight into the camera lens. There was not the slightest hint of fear or penitence in those young eyes.

As McCabe grew older the press covered his crimes not because of his youth but because of the appalling nature of his crimes. McCabe didn't just kill people, he used them, hurt them, and then got rid of them, as if they were nothing more than garbage. His disregard for the sanctity of human life was so obvious, so cavalier, it was breathtaking, even to a seasoned cop like Cassidy.

The peak of Peter McCabe's press coverage must have been the long think piece about him that had appeared in *Rolling Stone* a few years before.

In an attempt to crown a successor to Charles Manson, the magazine had profiled him in some depth. The article was called "Peter McCabe: Inside the Mind of a Sociopath." It was accompanied by a dramatic photo of McCabe in his prison cell. The picture had been touched up and dodged, until there was a greenish cast to McCabe's skin, a tone that reflected the institutional color of the prison cell. But no amount of darkroom tricks could obscure that defiant look, the one that Cassidy had already seen in the older picture, the one taken fifteen years before.

"McCabe has escaped twice," Cassidy said, reading from the article. "The second time he took two guards hostage, buried them alive, and used their uniforms and IDs to make his getaway."

Frank nodded. "I remember that. They found the guards alive, though, didn't they?"

"One of them," Cassidy replied. He didn't bother with the rest of the *Rolling Stone* article, flipping by it to a glossy forensic photograph, a picture of the guard who did not survive McCabe's escape. The corpse had been buried deep enough that the man's eyes, nose, and mouth were stuffed with dark brown dirt.

"Ah, Jesus, . . ." said Cassidy, turning the page quickly. But the image stayed in his head, as if it had been fixed there. He looked out the window, trying to erase the horrific image from his mind.

They were traveling through a deep, dark forest, the trees towering over the road, the light blocked by branches a hundred feet above them. A few shafts cut through the gloom, slanting, gleaming shafts that fell in diagonal bars across the car and the road. As they moved forward the bars of light strobed through the window. It was like driving through a vast cathedral.

Cassidy could not forget that guard. He could not forget that look in McCabe's eyes. He had seen evil, depravity, and corruption in a thousand different forms, but he had never seen that coldness before, that glacial indifference. He could sense that it went deep. It was in McCabe's genes.

He looked over at Frank. Connor was staring straight ahead. He did not appear to be seeing the roads, the trees, anything that was within the line of his sight. If he was thinking about McCabe he gave no sign of it. His jaw was set, his hands firm on the wheel.

Cassidy knew he had to say what was on his mind. "This is a mistake, Frank. Not McCabe . . . don't use him. There has to be somebody else. Anybody but McCabe."

Frank Connor was silent for a full mile before replying.

"It's the only choice I have." He looked over at Cassidy, a quick glance. "You know that."

They had reached the exit for Pelican Bay and Frank turned for it.

"I appreciate what you're doing for me, Captain," said Connor, turning off the highway. The ramp curved down toward the water and they could see the small community of Crescent City nestled on the coastline below them. Connor said all he could, as if his thanks would somehow make this all right.

"Yeah," said Cassidy. "I know." He did not say what he was really thinking: that getting mixed up with an unfeeling son of a bitch like Peter McCabe could only lead to disaster.

There had been a time when the goal of prison confinement had been rehabilitation, but arrest rates rose and crime became a political issue—getting tough on crime frequently meant getting tough on prisoners, who, in the popular imagination, "had things easy."

The mission of many American prisons had changed. Rehabilitation was a thing of the past. Incapacitation and deterrence became the primary objectives of penitentiaries all over the country. Hence the birth of a place like Pelican Bay.

It did not look like the high security facility it was. The prison was a simple building, two low, concrete blockhouses intersecting to form a gray cement X set in the middle of a vast clearing deep in the dense Malarky Forest. The compound was surrounded by a fourteen-foot-high skein of electrified razor wire, punctuated at intervals by glassed-in guard towers.

The philosophy behind prisoner control at Pelican Bay had been pioneered at Alcatraz, further developed at the federal pen in Marion, Illinois, but perfected at Pelican Bay. Prisoners were kept in a state called, officially, "indefinite administrative segregation," but it was something that guards and inmates alike called "permanent lockdown."

Those felons violent enough to warrant incarceration at Pelican Bay experienced almost no personal, face-to-face contact with other people, not even with prison staff. Virtually all day-to-day monitoring was done by television camera, and prisoners sat idle in their cells, constantly monitored by video and microphone. Corrections officers viewed them from control booths inside the prison and issued commands through loudspeakers.

In other prisons, inmates worked at maintenance jobs to earn money for privileges, but there was no work at Pelican Bay. There were no educational classes, no church services, practically no interaction at all. There was one hour of exercise in the yard a day—and that was the extent of interaction between inmates. The cells themselves were without windows, so that was the only time any of them saw the light of day.

Lawsuits had been brought against Pelican Bay, proceedings brought by prisoners and groups concerned with prisoners' rights. The constitutional guarantee against cruel and unusual punishment was cited; some inmates strove to have themselves declared political prisoners, citing a European report which stated that incarceration at Pelican Bay was inhumane and amounted to a basic contravention of human rights.

But through the protests and the lawsuits Pelican Bay had prevailed. It was the hardest time a criminal could do and only the most hardened, unreachable cases ever saw the inside of it.

Pelican Bay may have been a labyrinth of rules and regulations, but there was no control over what went on inside the minds of the prisoners. Such management was not considered necessary—most of the men sent to Pelican Bay, no matter how strong or feared they might have been on the outside, found that the regimentation and lack of contact with other human beings wore them down. They did not become docile—far from it—but they failed to harness or channel their anger and hostility. They did not look beyond the next day, the next petty infringement, the next rule they could break.

That was not McCabe's way. He was not a model prisoner—he was not afraid of a fight if he could get into one—but he took a longer view of incarceration. He did not vegetate, but kept his mind alive reading, thinking, writing, planning. He maintained his body as well, working out vigorously in his cell, hour after hour, every day, without interruption.

McCabe could do five hundred push-ups without stopping, the muscles in his back rippling like steel cord, his body gleaming with sweat, even in the poor light of the single bulb in the cage in the ceiling high above his head. He worked on himself with the intensity of a boxer, a man not content just to beat an opponent, but to *punish* him, demolish him, as well. His arms worked like pistons pushing his taut body up and down, his eyes fixed on a puddle of sweat that had dripped from his forehead and pooled on the floor of the cell.

The Spartan concrete box that contained Peter McCabe's body could not restrain his mind. The single shelf above the small counter that served as a desk was packed with books—volumes on everything from Spinoza to computers—and McCabe had read every word of every one. McCabe had used the printed word to escape from Pelican Bay. He had passed through the portal of imprisonment and into a world of his own making, a realm of mental and physical rigor where he was the absolute leader.

The thick plate of Plexiglas set in the door slid open and a guard looked in at McCabe as he pushed himself through his exercise regimen. The corrections officer stared at him for a moment, the look on his face suggesting that he regarded McCabe with the same loathing and respect he might show to a poisonous snake.

''McCabe,'' said the guard.

But the prisoner ignored him, shifting his weight

onto one arm, doing the rest of his push-ups with only one hand on the floor.

"McCabe."

But Peter McCabe would not be pushed and he would not be rushed. It was only when he had reached a figure he held in his head that he stopped and looked toward the opening in the thick steel door.

"What?"

"You have a visitor," the guard said, his voice sullen. "Put your clothes on."

McCabe's face registered nothing. He was not expecting a visitor, but he showed no surprise. In all his time in Pelican Bay he had never even *had* a visitor—yet his face showed no pleasure nor even a measure of curiosity or interest.

He merely nodded and slipped an orange prison jumpsuit over his taut body. Then he stepped up to the door and slid his hands through the slot the guard had opened. Shackles snapped around his wrists. The door swung open and leg irons were ratcheted into place, closing tight around his ankles.

"Okay," said the guard, moving him out into the corridor. "You know the drill. . . ."

Frank Connor had been in prisons before, a lot of them, but he had never been in one like Pelican Bay. In most houses of detention, even well-run, well-ordered ones, the noise was constant. The shouting of prisoners from cell to cell, from tier to tier, the blare of radios and television sets, the bellowed stentorian orders of guards—the noise echoed on the hard walls day and night. Pelican Bay was as silent as a crypt.

Other prisons were dirty, their floors littered with bits of paper, food, cigarette butts, spots of spit and other fluids. In other prisons, vermin was everywhere—cockroaches, rats, and mice thrived on the filth. Pelican Bay was as spotless as a hospital.

From a gallery above the corridor, guards looked down on Frank as he walked with an assistant warden named Tyman toward the single visiting room in the entire facility.

"I have to warn you," said Tyman, "McCabe is dangerous. He's already killed one prisoner here and crippled another."

"I know that," Connor replied.

"But more than that," Tyman continued, "more than the physical danger—we more or less have taken care of that, you'll see what I mean—McCabe is very sharp. Real smart. And he likes to fuck with you. That's his favorite thing, I think. I get the impression it's a more fun way of inflicting pain."

Frank nodded. "I know. I read the file and the psychological profile."

Tyman sort of laughed and shook his head, small gestures that suggested that Peter McCabe could not be summed up in a file and psychological profile.

They were approaching a thick steel door, stenciled with six-inch red letters: SOLITARY HOUSING UNIT.

"This is where we keep the problems," said Tyman, as if the other inmates of Pelican Bay were pussycats compared to the *real* hard cases like McCabe.

The steel door slid open and they stepped into the narrow passage that separated the Solitary Housing Unit from the rest of the prison. In the gallery above them were two guards, both of whom carried heavy FMC riot guns, pieces of handheld artillery that fired large shells at very high velocity. A couple of those unloaded into the tight quarters of that corridor would reduce to bloody shreds anyone trying to make an escape. In prison parlance these constricted passages, built-in choke points, were known as "kill zones."

Beyond the next set of sliding doors was a silent, well-lit room. In the middle of it was a rectangular stainless steel table, as government-issue a piece of furniture as Frank could imagine. Sitting at it was Peter McCabe.

The table might have been ordinary, but there was nothing commonplace about the chair the man was sitting in. It was made from bulky steel, the legs and arms twice as thick as usual, making the chair extremely heavy and difficult to move. McCabe was strapped into it: metal bands secured his wrists to the arms, his ankles were locked to the legs, and a wide metal band like a steel cummerbund restrained his waist. Peter McCabe could hardly move a muscle, yet there was something about this man that somehow managed to make this odd contraption, a special chair for violent prisoners, a piece of furniture that belonged more properly in the last century, into a throne. McCabe sat there like a potentate.

Frank took a seat across from him, then half turned and looked over his shoulder at Tyman.

"You don't have to stay."

The guard shrugged and nodded and left. Truth was, he didn't *want* to stay.

Frank Connor turned to face Peter McCabe and for a moment or two there was complete silence as the two men studied each other, each taking the measure of the other. Frank could see scars on McCabe's face, but he could tell that they were deeper than anything inflicted by any weapon. His was a face untouched by love—Peter McCabe did not love and no one had ever loved him. The anger, the iron determination, the strong will—they were apparent in the resolute set of his mouth. Less obvious, but lurking, was the enormous intelligence of this man, as if it were something he had to keep hidden, a weapon in reserve; but it was there too, in the eyes.

McCabe read Frank Connor in an instant. The man was scared, but not in the physical sense, not the way the guards were. He did not shrink from contact with him, the way other prisoners in the yard did, afraid for their lives. McCabe could sense the fear, but he could not discern its origin. For once, he was intrigued.

Frank filled in the blanks immediately. "My son has leukemia," he said, his voice loud and strong, as if saying the dread words would show that he was not afraid of them. "He will die without a bone marrow transplant. He will die soon. . . ."

McCabe's face was a mask, betraying nothing. The plight of a desperately ill child meant absolutely nothing to him.

"He's nine years old," Connor said, as if this piece of information would make a difference.

"What's his name?"

"Matthew Connor." Frank shrugged. "Matt. . . ."

McCabe understood immediately, his brain deciphering and interpreting the information in an instant. He nodded slowly.

"I see. . . . And somehow I've been identified as a compatible donor for Matt."

Frank Connor found the sound of his son's name on McCabe's lips oddly intimate and disconcerting.

"And," McCabe continued, "I gather I have somehow volunteered for this operation."

"That's what I've been told," Connor replied. It was not exactly the truth. When he had explained his plight to the warden of Pelican Bay and wondered aloud if McCabe would make the donation, the warden had replied: "He'll do what he's told."

"How?" McCabe asked.

"How what?"

"How was I identified?" McCabe said, a trace of impatience in his voice. "How did you find out I was a genetic match for your son?"

Frank shifted uneasily in his chair, a little piece of body language not lost on Peter McCabe. "I don't know," he replied with a shrug, hoping the gesture explained something. "I guess the computer—"

McCabe cut him off. "What am I? Some long lost brother of yours? Is that what brought you here?" He laughed out loud. "Maybe you talked to Dad. How is the old bastard?"

"I was told you volunteered," Frank Connor said, his voice flat and emotionless.

Peter McCabe stared at him for a long moment, then, without warning, he raised his voice and shouted. "Officers! We're finished here!"

Frank jumped, startled and confused. "What? What's wrong? What did I—"

"You're lying to me, Frank," said McCabe in a normal tone of voice. For an instant, Connor saw real hatred flash in those eyes.

McCabe shouted again, "Officers!"

The door behind them started to open with a warning buzz. Frank tried to fight down the panic rising inside of him.

"Don't do this," he whispered urgently. "McCabe, please—"

McCabe leaned as far forward in the chair as he could, his eyes burning. "Okay . . . last chance, Frank. How was I identified, Frank?"

"I told you," said Frank quickly, desperately. "By computer match. The computer picked you out. It's the truth."

"One analysis of my DNA was done in March of 1988. It was sealed by a federal court order," McCabe spat out. "How did you get access to it?"

Tyman, along with two other guards, entered the room. "That was fast," Tyman said. There seemed to be something like glee in his voice, a sense that he was pleased that Peter McCabe had proved he could not be a useful member of society.

"I broke into the FBI computer system," Frank whispered. "It was the last place I could think of to look."

McCabe nodded and smiled. "That constitutes illegal entry, doesn't it, Frank? Breaking into a computer like that. A violation of federal statutes, not to mention police protocol. Am I correct about that, Frank?"

Frank swallowed hard and nodded. "Yes."

McCabe sat back in the chair, as relaxed as if he were at a dinner party. "I'm sorry, officers," he said to Tyman and the guards. "False alarm. We're okay here. Aren't we, Frank?"

Tyman looked at McCabe, then down at Frank Connor. "You sure?"

Frank nodded. "Fine. It's fine."

The three COs exchanged scowls, but retreated. McCabe did not speak again until the steel doors had slid closed again.

McCabe sat up straight in the restraint chair and looked at Frank like a reproving schoolteacher. "Gee, what would happen if your commanding officer knew about this? It would be pretty serious, wouldn't it, Frank? It would *not* look good."

"I'd be thrown out of the department." Mentally he added: *At least.*

McCabe smiled. He knew that of course. "Tell me, did you do it yourself, Frank? Or did you have a friend? Someone who really knows his way around computers? Some hacker friend of yours, maybe."

Frank could think of no reason why he should give Nate up to a felon like McCabe. "I did it myself," he said without hesitation.

"How? Explain in precise detail how you learned the passwords and circumvented the C-2 internal security system." He spoke as if delivering a question for an exam.

This time Frank did hesitate. He knew it was pointless trying to bullshit this man. "I have a friend," he said finally. "He knew how to do all that."

"That's twice you lied to me," said McCabe. "You've only been here a couple of minutes and you've lied to me twice. Please don't do it again."

Frank was beginning to understand the warnings he had received from Tyman. In a matter of minutes, McCabe had managed to turn the tables on him. He had caught him in the commission of a federal offense, he had forced him to implicate an associate. McCabe had put Connor on the defensive.

"This donating of my marrow," McCabe asked, cocking his chin, "what does it entail?"

Frank felt the earth slide back under his feet. He was on steadier ground, but McCabe had put it there—and he could yank it out from under him at will. "They'll insert a needle into the bone of your hip, extract some marrow, and infuse it into Matt."

"And will I feel pain?" McCabe asked—as if he gave a *damn* about pain.

"You will be anesthetized," Connor replied. He had given this spiel so many times he could have recited it in his sleep. "Afterward you'll have some discomfort"—Doctors never called it pain; it was always discomfort—"but you'll be up and around again—"

McCabe nodded quickly. "Yeah, yeah . . . I'm up and around the next day. I know all that. Up and around and back here the next day. Back here." His eyes flicked around the room to underscore his point. "Right where we are now. So . . ."

Frank shrugged. "So?" He had said his piece. It was all up to Peter McCabe now.

"So what do I get out of it?" McCabe asked. "What's in it for me? Besides an eight-hour round-trip drive down to San Francisco and back, shackled inside a prison van?'' He smiled. ''You know, I don't think they'd even let me look out the window. . . . So you tell me, Frank, why should I even bother?''

Frank Connor stared at him for a moment. To him the answer was obvious. ''Because you get to save my son's life,'' he said.

''And why do I care about your son's life?'' McCabe shot back. ''I take lives. I don't save them. A couple of them weren't much older than Matt. Am I supposed to get some kind of redemption in the eyes of God? Is that what you're offering me, Frank?''

''Do you want redemption?''

''Do you think I do?'' McCabe asked quickly.

Frank Connor raised an eyebrow and half smiled. ''You brought it up.''

Frank had scored his first point; McCabe knew it and he acknowledged the little cut with a smile of his own. He appreciated a worthy adversary—but within proper limits of course.

McCabe shook his head slowly. ''Don't try to get inside my head, Frank. If I want you in, I'll invite you in. Understand?''

''I'm sorry,'' said Frank evenly. ''I thought you were opening the door.'' He sounded as if he was being genuinely apologetic, even respectful, but McCabe thought he detected a rejoinder to his own attempts at manipulation. It had been a long time since he had encountered a worthy adversary—he wondered if he was getting a little rusty at playing the mind game.

McCabe grinned across the table. "To answer your question, then: I don't care about your son. I don't care about you or your God."

On an intellectual level Frank figured he knew this already. But it was chilling—even frightening—to hear it put in so matter-of-fact a manner.

"I killed," McCabe continued. "I killed: two kids, a man in a store, a woman with a hat, a guard in the ground. Boom, boom. That was that."

Frank had the feeling that if McCabe's hands had not been restrained he would be ticking these lives off as if they were no more important than items on a list of groceries.

"Those deaths . . . they were real. Those things happened, and you know what? I cannot make myself feel bad about it. I cannot imagine a God who would care." He fixed his eyes on Frank's face. "I put my faith in the power of my own mind, which is, after all, the only thing I own after half a life of incarceration."

"I can appreciate that."

McCabe shook his head. "No, you can't," he said. "And don't even try."

"How do you—"

"The difference between us is quite simple," said McCabe. "There's no great void. The difference is that *you* believe, Frank. In God, the social contract, paternal love. You believe in those things, don't you?"

"Yes, I do." Frank was not embarrassed to admit that he did believe in those things.

"Yes." McCabe nodded. "Whereas I go it alone. That's all."

"Alone?"

"That's right," said McCabe, nodding again. "Without badge or backup. Without the law behind me. And you don't do that. Or do you?"

It seemed to Frank that the intensity of McCabe's gaze had been heightened by a notch or two. He didn't wait for an answer—it was plain that he thought he knew it already.

"You know what I always admire about the police?" McCabe asked.

"You admire something about the police?"

"Oh yes. I've learned a lot from the police over the years. . . . I learned how to lie from the police. Cops are master liars. They will tell you any lie they can to make you do what they want."

"I'm telling you the truth."

"You're also telling me that there is some kind of divine redemption in taking a narcotic and having a little bone marrow sucked painlessly out of your hip. That's the bill of goods being sold here, isn't it, Frank?"

"We can hold back the anesthetic, make it hurt if you want."

"A sense of humor," said McCabe without a trace of humor in his voice. "I like that. Perhaps you share my amusement at the irony that now, after being locked up all these years, I'm given another opportunity to kill a child—a cop's kid, at that—and all I have to do is stay here."

"I don't see the humor," said Frank slowly.

"Come on, Frank," said McCabe as if trying to jolly him along. "Don't get locked in your subjective feelings. I'm the prisoner, I'm the one shackled, tied down, locked up—but you're the helpless one. You have to see some irony in that, don't you?'' He ended his remarks with a little smile, as though he were inviting Frank to join in enjoying the little joke.

Frank felt the frustration of powerlessness surge through him, followed by a flame of hot, sharp anger. He was on the verge of losing what little patience he had—and he knew that if he did so he would be playing straight into McCabe's hands. He swallowed hard and tried to calm himself down.

''Let's get down to business, okay?'' Frank hoped he sounded as if he was in a hurry and untroubled by anything that McCabe had said.

But McCabe met him head on. ''Okay, business: What makes you worth my mercy?''

Frank played the only card he had and hoped that his adversary had a shred of humanity left. ''My son is dying. Only you can save him.''

McCabe tried to suppress the little smile that came to his face, but he couldn't. Frank could not tell if the smile was an acknowledgment of the power that the criminal held over him or if there were other, more private reasons for his mirth.

''I didn't ask why your son deserved mercy, Frank,'' McCabe replied. ''Of course *he* does—he's an innocent child. What kind of creatures are we if we don't show mercy to a child? . . .'' McCabe didn't even try to keep the note of irony from his voice. ''The question I asked was, what makes *you* worthy?''

Frank dropped his guard and really thought about the question. In the months since Matt's diagnosis he had asked himself and heaven the same question over and over again: Why me? Why did it have to be his son afflicted with this awful disease? Why had this burden been selected for him to carry?

Now, here it was, the same question put another way. Why *not* Frank Connor? He was silent for several moments, then he looked McCabe square in the eye. ''I am not worthy,'' he said finally.

McCabe was not impressed with the sudden burst of introspection. ''Nice answer. But why not? Why aren't you worthy? Why don't you deserve to save your son? I mean, have you been a good father to the boy?''

Frank Connor's shoulders slumped and he looked down at the steel table. ''I've tried to be.''

But McCabe shrugged off that answer, as if it was standard parenting boilerplate. ''Yes, well, I bet even my dad would say that. He beat the shit out of me every day, but, hey, he tried.''

''I never hit Matt.'' The response sounded defensive and inadequate. And both men knew it.

''I'm sure you didn't,'' McCabe replied. ''And neither did my dad. He never got the chance. He walked out when I was three years old. I never knew the man. Wouldn't recognize him if he walked in here now.''

Frank wondered if this was a chink in McCabe's armor. ''And that put you on a bad road, didn't it?''

McCabe cackled at bit at that, contemptuous of Frank's amateurish stab at psychoanalysis. ''Please, Frank, spare me the bullshit, will you? It's beneath you.'' He paused a moment as if considering which tack to take next. ''What about the boy's mother?'' he asked after a while. ''Where is she?''

"She's dead."

"Are you responsible for her death in any way?" McCabe asked, sounding as unfeeling as a census form. He didn't care which bruises he pressed or how much they hurt Frank Connor.

Frank looked up sharply, then saw the bright merriment in McCabe's eyes and realized that he was being made fun of, toyed with to spare a psychopath an otherwise boring, institutional morning.

"She died in a car wreck," said Frank sharply. "But you knew that already, didn't you?"

"Yes, I know that."

And he was convinced that McCabe had, somehow, figured out that his wife had died suddenly, tragically. Maybe McCabe didn't know the specifics, but he had *known.*

"Did you love her?"

Frank exhaled heavily. "Not enough," he admitted. "Not in the right way."

"Is *that* why you aren't worthy?" McCabe asked. He sounded much like a district attorney building an airtight case.

But suddenly Frank was hardly listening. He was looking down again, lost in his own miasma of miserable thoughts. The weight of the guilt he carried was almost staggering. It was not the first time he had wondered if he carried some curse, some hex that afflicted anyone who ever got close to him.

McCabe shook his head. "A dead wife and a kid with cancer. I'd wonder about myself too. It's only natural, Frank."

Connor realized too late that he had made a mistake: He had let McCabe in, made him privy to his most private doubts and fears—potent weapons in the hardened hands of a man like Peter McCabe.

"Listen, I didn't—" he started to say, protesting, attempting to muster a defense.

But McCabe had the upper hand now and he pressed his advantage. "What was the marriage like, Frank? Did you ever cheat on her?"

"No!"

McCabe adopted a roguish smile, and if he had been sitting next to Connor, if his hands had not been chained to a chair, he would have given him a good-natured, guy-to-guy elbow in the ribs. "C'mon . . . good-looking guy like you, Frank—"

Then, abruptly, he turned prosecutorial again. "And what was her blood/alcohol level at the time of the accident?" He had taken a fragment of information and worked on it. McCabe had no idea if Frank Connor's wife had been driving drunk when she died in her accident—but she might have been. It was a stab in the dark, but a stab nonetheless.

And it stung. Frank jumped to his feet, fury pulsing through him. He turned, ready to storm out of there, desperate to get away from McCabe, his face, his taunting voice. . . . But then he realized he couldn't leave, he didn't have the luxury of giving in to his anger. Far more was at stake here than his own pride, his own sense of self-worth. It was just as McCabe had made plain—there was no freedom here for him. Frank forced himself to sit down again.

"See how you can master yourself when you have to?" McCabe said.

But Frank had already had more than enough. "Will you do it?" He ran his hand through his hair as he tried hard to compose himself. "Will you give my son your bone marrow?"

"I'll think about it and let you know." McCabe sounded like the soul of insouciance.

Frank shook his head. "No. Not good enough. I have to know right now."

"Why?"

Frank didn't want to have to explain himself any further, but his only hope was to tell the truth and hope for the best—McCabe would accept nothing less than the truth, even if he had to wrench it out of him.

"Because I haven't told him yet—I haven't told Matt that his cancer is back. He went through chemo—he was the bravest human being—man, woman, or child—I ever saw. But when he went into remission . . ."

Frank breathed deep, fighting down the impulse to give in to tears. "When he went into remission he wouldn't let himself celebrate because he's smart enough to know his odds."

He looked up hoping to see a glimmer of compassion on McCabe's features, but the man's face was impossible to read.

"Now, when I tell him the leukemia is back, and when I tell him that he won't live unless he gets a bone marrow transplant, I want to tell him I've found a donor. I want to give him hope."

"To make it easier for you," said McCabe pointedly. "Right?"

"No," said Frank sharply. "To make it easier for him. And to save his life." He looked McCabe in the eye. "So tell me now."

"Well, Frank . . . since you have to know right now . . . my answer is no." Peter McCabe sounded like some old guy thinking he was being canny turning down the first offer on a used car.

All the color drained from Frank's face and he felt as if he had been kicked in the stomach. He could not move; he just sat there, his hands clenched on the edge of the table, as if steadying himself.

McCabe had a wicked little smile on his face as he sang out: "*Offffff-i-cers! . . . Time to goooooo-oh!*"

chapter 2

When Samantha Hawkins became a doctor she chose as her specialty the area of medicine considered one of the toughest, most demanding fields of them all: pediatric oncology.

To spend your days caring for kids afflicted with cancer meant dealing with a constant stream of conflicting emotions. To nurse a six-year-old back from the brink of death brought the most incredible highs; but watching as a child succumbed slowly and painfully to neuroblastoma or lymphoma was emotionally devastating.

Doctors who took on this demanding specialty had to have the compassion and forbearance of a saint, mixed with the toughness and hardheadedness of a Marine. It was a combination of characteristics that did not come along every day, but Samantha Hawkins had it.

She was a no-nonsense woman of about thirty-five, pretty, but paid little attention to her looks. Her work, her patients were paramount, and the long hours she put in on the cancer wards at San Francisco Memorial Hospital could wear her down to pure exhaustion.

Hawkins's work was never done and sometimes she felt she was being pulled in a dozen different directions at once. It was a stress-filled, intense, demanding way to make a living, but one that she would not have traded for a cushy practice in a rich suburb or a stable of high-profile plastic surgery clients that would have made her rich beyond belief.

The publicity surrounding the case of Matthew Connor meant nothing to her. She did not play to the cameras, she did not grant interviews. To her, Matt was a desperately ill child who needed her help. That was all that mattered, and if a little notoriety would help in finding a donor she was not against it, as long as the public eye stayed firmly fixed on her little patient and his grave condition.

Like everyone else connected to Matt's case, Hawkins's hopes had risen when she heard that Frank Connor had located that single person who might be a donor match. And, like everyone else, her optimism had crashed when Peter McCabe had turned down the chance to do a little good.

She was on the phone at a nurses' station on the cancer floor of Memorial Hospital when she saw Frank Connor step out of an elevator and make his way down the corridor toward his son's room.

"I'll call you back," she announced abruptly and slammed down the phone, hurrying after Connor. "Mr. Connor, wait!" She noticed that he carried a gaily wrapped present in one hand, something large and heavy.

Frank turned and looked at her blankly. It took a moment to place her, not because she wasn't known to him, but because he was so preoccupied with thoughts of Matt that right then he probably would not have recognized his own face in a mirror.

He shook his head quickly. "Dr. Hawkins. Sorry, I was . . ." He shrugged and did his best to smile. "A lot on my mind, I'm afraid."

Hawkins waved away the apology. "I just heard about Peter McCabe declining to be a donor." A look on her face suggested that though she had seen a lot of human suffering she was never unaffected by it.

"We'll see," Frank replied.

"What do you mean?" Hawkins looked puzzled by this. As far as she knew, Peter McCabe had turned him down flat and that was that.

"Maybe he'll change his mind," said Frank. "Is Matt in his room?"

Samantha Hawkins shook her head. "No, he's up on six. Just some tests we wanted to run. He'll be done with them in a few minutes, though."

Frank nodded, but continued to plod slowly down the corridor toward his son's room.

Hawkins had something on her mind, something she had been meaning to bring up with Frank Connor, but she had never been quite sure of the moment. Of course, she had learned long ago that there was never a right time to start preparing for the death of a child.

"Mr. Connor . . ."

Frank stopped, turned, and looked at her. "Yes?"

Hawkins breathed deep. "Mr. Connor, one thing you learn by having a specialty in which you lose most of your patients . . . you also have to care for the family, the ones who live on—"

"Matt is going to make it," he said. Frank Connor had to believe that. His wife was dead. If Matt died then there would *be* no family.

"We won't give up hope," Dr. Hawkins replied noncommittally, but she was also a realist. "We have to face facts. He's got blood in his urine, his creatine levels are up. You have to understand that without the bone marrow transplant, he has very little time." Frank Connor winced at her words and she felt the pain in her own heart. But she knew there was no point in sugarcoating this, the most bitter of pills.

"You may want someone to talk to," said Hawkins, pressing on. "The hospital has counselors who can help you."

The bones in Connor's face seemed to sag a little, but there was anger in his dark eyes. "A counselor? For what? So I can adjust to my son dying? I don't want to adjust to that. I want to get him that transplant." He paused a moment and shook his head slowly. "I don't mean to get mad at you, Doctor. You've been great. I know you've done everything you can."

He didn't say what was *really* on his mind. The thought that Peter McCabe was up there in Pelican Bay, proprietor of the one substance that could save the life of his son, refusing to give it up so he could play some mind game with a cop he didn't even know . . . Frank felt his anger intensify. He wishcd he had grabbed McCabe by the throat and extracted the damn marrow himself. Connor wiped a hand across his face. "I'm sorry. . . ."

"Look," Dr. Hawkins replied, "I don't usually get involved on this level, but the EC has a bone marrow registry—"

"The EC?"

"European Community, in Belgium."

Frank nodded. "Right."

"The registry is based at EC headquarters in Belgium. I have some colleagues in Brussels; maybe I could get us access to it. The registry is for EC members, but in an extreme case they might be helpful. . . ." She shrugged. "I know it's not much, but it's something. In case McCabe doesn't change his mind. Okay?"

Frank Connor nodded vaguely, as if he hadn't quite caught everything Hawkins had said. "Okay, okay . . . I appreciate it, Doctor. Thank you. Do you think I can see Matt now?"

Matthew Connor was a lively, intelligent kid, with the same black hair and dark eyes of his father. The long day of tests had worn him down, but he was not completely out. It took a lot to squeeze all the energy out of a nine-year-old boy, even a gravely ill one.

As two nurses wheeled his gurney back into his room, Matt busied himself with the pile of slim wooden coffee stirrers in his lap, makeshift toys he had picked up from the nurses' lounge.

". . . Now, can you build a rocket ship out of these

coffee stirrers without glue or any other adhesive?'' he asked the women.

With brisk efficiency the two nurses lifted him off the gurney—he was light, a slim envelope of skin and bone—and placed him in his bed, arranging the pillows and straightening the sheets.

''You mean, make something that holds together without glue?'' one of the nurses asked. She looked over at the balsa wood Spad biplane, now complete. That had been made with glue.

Matt nodded enthusiastically. ''That's right. Something that holds together. Strong enough so you can pick it up and it won't fall apart.''

The nurses played along. It was the least they could do for this sunny-faced kid. ''I doubt it,'' said one.

''I know I can't,'' said the other. ''Talk about a klutz.''

Of course, that was what Matt had hoped they would say. ''Okay, watch. . . .'' He picked up a handful of the little wooden sticks and began bending and folding them, placing them just so, allowing for opposing tensions to hold the structure together. Much to the surprise of the nurses his agile little fingers were assembling something that did look like a rocket ship. He was almost finished with it when his father walked in.

Matt looked up as Frank came into the room, delighted to see a familiar face. ''Hey Dad, look!''

''Wow! That's terrific,'' said Frank, examining the structure, smiling with pride. He had seen his son pull off little feats of engineering like this before, but everything about his son delighted him. As usual, he found himself marveling at his spirit, considering the ordeal he had already undergone and the further trials that his child was facing.

"I guess he's going to grow up to be an architect," said one of the nurses. She knew, of course, that there was very little chance of Matt growing up at all, but she could not face that fact, even if the child could.

"Uh-uh." Matt shook his head vigorously. "I'm not going to be an architect. I'm going to design interstellar spacecraft."

The unintended grimness of the speculation as to what Matt would be when he grew up cast a pall over the room. The nurses felt it and hastily said their good-byes, leaving father and son alone.

Frank rested a hip against the high bed and smoothed his son's hair. "How do you feel?" he asked.

Abruptly, Matt stopped fiddling with the latticework of wooden strips and lay back on the mound of pillows. The animation drained from his face and he looked wan and weary.

"Not so good," he said. "They ran about a billion tests today." He sighed heavily. "And the etopacide always wipes me out, you know that."

The cocktail of drugs that Matt ingested every day left him weak and debilitated. Frank smiled and nodded sympathetically.

"Here," he said, handing over the present. "Maybe this will make you feel a little better."

Matt stripped off the bright paper wrapping and his eyes brightened as he realized what his father had brought him. If money could cure Matt Connor he would have been up and about months ago. Frank had dropped a hundred dollars on a giant coffee-table book, a fat volume filled with dozens of beautiful color pictures of classic airplanes in flight.

When Matt saw the lavishly illustrated book, his eyes brightened and he seemed to rally for a moment, pushing aside the fatigue. Frank saw that small rally and figured his money was well spent.

"Oh, Dad, wow! Thanks!" Matt started to turn the thick pages. It was a chronological history of flight, starting with the first crude airplanes and working up to the present day. Frank sat on the edge of the bed and looked at the pictures over his son's shoulder.

"Look," said Matt, examining one of the illustrations closely. "Here's a Spad. Just like the one I built. This gives me some ideas for painting it."

There were other World War I planes—a Nieuport, a Sopwith Pup, an SE 5—then a large collection of Second World War vintage.

"P-51 Mustang!" Matt said enthusiastically, pointing out the long nose and under-fuselage air scoop. "It kicks! It was the best fighter of World War II, bar none. Better than anything Germany had."

He turned a few more pages, looking at a P-47 Thunderbolt, a P-38 Lightning and a P-40 Warhawk, the plane made famous by the Flying Tigers.

He looked back at his father, his face gleaming. "They were named after tiger sharks, not tigers the cats." He clipped forward a few pages. Then he stopped, looking at a vast B-17 Flying Fortress.

"The cancer is back, isn't it, Dad." Matt spoke

so casually that Frank was caught completely off guard. There was nothing he could do but tell the truth.

"Yes."

Matt said nothing, letting a few pages of the book slip through his fingers, then he stopped and pointed. "F-111," he said. "That was the swing wing—"

"But I think we've found a donor for a bone marrow transplant." That was the truth too—technically, if nothing else.

Matt nodded to himself, then moved on to a picture of an F-4 Phantom swooping down from a bank of high clouds. He did not seem excited by his father's news, but guarded, as though his hopes had been raised too high in the past for him to be taken in again.

"Really? Is he compatible?"

"He is compatible," said Frank. "And he's thinking it over, whether he's going to do it or not. It's kind of a big decision for this guy."

This appeared to puzzle Matt a little bit. His brow furrowed, but he did not take his eyes off the pages of the book in his lap. "You mean he might not want to do the transplant?"

Doubts and uncertainties do not enter the moral universe of a child—"right is right and wrong is wrong" is a very strictly defined concept—so the notion of *not* helping out someone who really needed help sounded strange and unfathomable.

"He'll do it," said Frank firmly. In his mind he was willing it to be so. But his insistence only seemed to suggest doubt. Matt continued to leaf through the book, but Frank could tell that his son was not paying as much attention as he had been.

"You know," Matt said, "even if he doesn't—"

"He will," Frank insisted. "He will do it, Matt. I swear to you."

But Matt persisted. "But even if he doesn't. Or if my body rejects the transplant"—his eyes flicked to his father's face—"because that does happen sometimes, doesn't it?"

Frank shrugged. "I—"

"Whatever," Matt continued. "I want you to know that it's okay, Dad. You did your best."

Frank Connor put a hand on his son's shoulder. "Don't worry, Matt. Okay?"

Matt closed the book and studied his father's face. "I just don't want you feeling guilty about any of this, Dad. That's all." He could see that his father was stunned, dazed by his words. Then, as if Matt thought this was more than his father could bear, he tried to soften his words. "Thank you, Dad . . . for trying so hard."

Frank could not speak. All he could do was enfold his son in a bear hug and hold him close, his head on his son's shoulder, doing his best to prevent him seeing the tears in his eyes.

chapter 3

It's a dirty little secret of the medical profession. Doctors and nurses—the people who are always wagging their fingers at their patients who smoke—are frequently closet smokers themselves. The pressure of hospital life is usually the cause, and most of them didn't smoke until after graduation from medical school, when the dangers of the habit had been well and truly—not to say graphically—inculcated. It was the frenzy and exhaustion of the internship that usually did it, and those who made it through those years without taking up smoking were generally in the clear.

Dr. Samantha Hawkins did not make it. Although every square inch of San Francisco Memorial Hospital was proclaimed a smoke-free environment (and large signs on the walls, posted, it seemed, every few feet in the corridors, bragged about that fact), Samantha Hawkins would sneak back to her office periodically and sneak a smoke, praying that no civilian entered during her furtive, forbidden pleasure. She wasn't worried about other med staffers—they might not necessarily approve, but she knew they would not say a word about it.

After leaving Frank Connor in the hallway outside his son's room, she walked quickly back to her office. She glanced at her watch, trying to figure out the time difference between San Francisco and Brussels, wondering if her old friend Etienne Vovelle would be in the office at what she took to be either 4 A.M. or 4 P.M.

Hawkins dialed the number, then, patting the pockets of her lab coat, found her cigarettes and lit one before the phone started ringing in Belgium.

Dr. Vovelle seemed surprised but pleased to hear from Samantha Hawkins. After a few moments of catching up, telling about their own careers and a little gossip about colleagues, they got down to the matter at hand. Hawkins's French was rusty and, while she could handle the news and gossip without too much trouble, she found that she had a little trouble with trying to translate the medical side of the conversation. Phrases like "a patient whose cells are positive for the enzyme terminal deoxynucleotidyl transferage" did not translate easily into the language of Proust and Rimbaud. She smoked as she talked and she could tell that Etienne was smoking too—of course, smoking was not a hanging offense in Europe, not yet anyway.

In the middle of the conversation, Samantha Hawkins saw that the second line on her phone began to blink insistently.

"*M'excuse, Etienne. Attends un moment, si'l te plaît.*" She pressed the button for the other line. "*Oui?* I mean, yes? . . . Yes, this is Dr. Hawkins." She listened a moment, then crushed out her cigarette, her eyes growing wider as she listened. . . .

Worn out by the medical procedures and tests, as well as the excitement and emotion of Frank's news about a possible donor, Matt had fallen asleep before his dinner tray arrived. The book was closed on his lap and his head rested against his father's shoulder, Frank scarcely daring to breathe for fear of disturbing his son. Connor did not sleep, but he had fallen into a deep, preoccupied reverie, free-associating about Matt, his illness, and the possibility of recovery.

He jumped when the door swung open. Dr. Hawkins saw that Matt was asleep and whispered, "Frank, pick up the phone. They're putting a call through to you."

There was a look on the doctor's face that suggested that this call might not only be urgent, but could be good news as well.

Frank snatched up the phone as it buzzed. "Frank Connor."

"Hello, Frank," said Peter McCabe amiably. "How's it going?"

Frank didn't even try to conceal the excitement in his voice. A call from McCabe could only mean one thing. "McCabe?"

The noise of the telephone and his father's voice had roused Matt. As he stirred, drifting toward consciousness, Frank stroked his hair.

"Gee, Frank," said McCabe with a laugh. "You wouldn't believe what I had to go through to get to use the phone. I had to plead with them—I had to tell them it was a life-or-death situation for a cop's kid." He was shackled to his chair and the phone was held to his ear by a guard. McCabe looked at the guard and winked, then chuckled. " 'Course, when I told them that, it pretty much did the trick."

The breath was locked in Frank's lungs. He was holding his breath in anticipation of what McCabe was going to say next. Surely he had called to volunteer his bone marrow—or was he just fooling around, finding one more way to twist the knife?

"So?" said Frank. That was all he dared say.

"I've changed my mind, Frank," said McCabe. "I'll do it."

Frank's knees seemed to buckle slightly and he bit his lip. Relief flowed through him like a drug. He tried to speak and found he could not.

"You there, Frank?"

"I'm here," he managed to say, his voice rough and hoarse.

"Indeed," McCabe continued. "So now we move into the area of quid pro quo. I will do this if, and only if, certain things are done for me."

Frank knew that he was in no position to make any deals. McCabe was going to have to do this out of the goodness—such as it was—of his heart, or not do it at all. He wondered if McCabe knew that too and had volunteered knowing he would not be able to make the precious donation. "Listen, I—"

"Just shut up and listen, please," said McCabe very calmly. "You will instruct the warden to give me back my smoking privileges, to reinstate my access to the prison library, to allow me four packets of sugar with my coffee . . . and to get me out of the box they call my cell and back into the general population.'' McCabe paused a moment. ''Did you get that, Frank? Or do you want me to run that by you again?''

In spite of himself, and notwithstanding the fact that the Department of Corrections would be loath to make any kind of deal with a man like Peter McCabe, Frank had snatched a piece of paper from Matt's bedside table and was scribbling down the demands.

Matt watched his father writing as if he were taking down the demands of kidnappers.

''I'll see what I can do,'' said Connor. Four sugars, some cigarettes, some books . . . even access to the other criminals in the yard . . . none of these things seemed to be worth withholding when measured against the life of a child. Frank was sure he would feel the same way about these few meaningless concessions even if the child were not his own.

''You see what you can do, Frank,'' McCabe continued, his words echoing Frank's own thoughts, ''because it would be kind of pathetic if for lack of cigarettes, sugar, and a library, your son had to die. Wouldn't it?''

''I don't have any control over the warden up there, McCabe,'' Frank said cautiously, careful not to promise anything. ''You know that as well as I do.''

''Hey, I have confidence in you,'' said McCabe, chuckling again. ''I bet you'll think of something. . . .

Now, is there anything you would like to tell me?''

The muscles in Frank's jaws clenched—but he knew it had to be said. ''Thanks.''

''Noted. Appreciated,'' McCabe replied. He was silent a moment, as if analyzing Frank's brief word of thanks. ''But there's something else, isn't there? A little hesitation there, maybe? Come on, you can tell me. What's bothering you, Frank?''

''You could have told me earlier.''

''I had to think it over,'' said McCabe. ''Besides, I wanted Matt to appreciate me. If you'd gone back from here and told him you'd found a donor, he'd be grateful to you. Now he's grateful to me.''

''That sounds a little bit like you're searching for redemption,'' said Frank quickly.

''Maybe, in a way.'' Frank could not tell if McCabe was being ironic or, for once, up front and honest about his motives. His tone of voice betrayed nothing, no hint. ''Help a kid. Help myself. Who knows, right, Frank?'' This time Connor could hear the sly smile that he knew was forming on McCabe's face.

''Who knows.'' Frank smiled too, as if they were enemies engaged in a duel—the cause of which only they knew, a secret between them.

''Come to think of it . . . how about putting Matt on the phone? I'd like to say hello to him. That would just make my day.'' McCabe was pushing again, looking to see how far he could go until a line was crossed and Frank started pushing back.

That was the line. Frank did not want his son to talk to Peter McCabe, as if real, live, personal interaction would somehow contaminate Matt. He felt as though exposure to McCabe's personality and persona would infect him in a way a piece of his body would not.

"He's . . . not here." Frank's voice was hollow and it would have been plain to anyone that he was lying, and doing it badly at that.

Of course, McCabe didn't buy it for a moment. "*Sure* he is, Frank. Come on. . . . You think I'm good enough to give him a little bit of my bone marrow, but not good enough to talk to him, do you?" McCabe's voice suddenly turned hard. "Put him on . . . before I change my mind and call off the whole thing."

Frank covered the mouthpiece of the receiver with his palm and did his best to force a smile onto his face. "Matt, the donor has agreed to do it. He wants to say hi to you."

Matt's face lit up like a neon sign, the incandescence of his smile betraying the fact that the adult stoicism he had been displaying earlier was something of a facade. He held out his hands for the phone.

"Let me talk to him, Dad."

Frank breathed deep. He knew he was going to hand over the phone, but he wanted his son to be prepared. "Matt, he's a . . ." There was no easy way to say this. "He's a man in prison. But he's going to help you. Maybe you could just say thank you to him."

Matt nodded and took the phone. "Hello?"

Peter McCabe was as comfortable and easygoing

as a department store Santa. ''Hi there, Matt,'' he said. ''How you feeling?''

''I guess a lot better now,'' Matt said earnestly. ''Thank you so much for what you're doing for me, sir. I really appreciate it.''

''Oh, I'm glad to help,'' said McCabe easily, as if it had never occurred to him to turn down the request. ''We haven't been introduced. My name is Peter. So you can just call me Pete.'' McCabe was incapable of *not* pushing the line. Even with a child. ''Uncle Pete. You call me Uncle Pete. Okay?''

Matt did not reply, clearly uncomfortable with the notion. McCabe sensed the child's discomfiture and tried to put him at his ease, but talking to a child was more difficult than he'd imagined. McCabe didn't like children. He hadn't liked children when *he* was a child.

''So . . . you're nine. What's that? Fourth grade, right? You like school?''

Without thinking, McCabe laughed. ''I fucking hated every minute of it!'' It was the kind of thing he would have said to some guy in a bar, some guy he was trying to get to know so he could lift the guy's wallet and the keys to his truck. Instantly McCabe realized he had said the wrong thing.

''Yes, sir,'' said Matt, sounding as noncommittal as he could manage.

''Not *sir*,'' McCabe insisted. ''Uncle Pete! I said, call me Uncle Pete.''

''But you're not my uncle,'' Matt replied, using that unassailable logic of a nine-year-old.

Frank snatched the phone from Matt's hand. ''That's it for now, McCabe. He needs to rest.''

"He sounds like a nice boy, Frank."

"He is."

"Well, that's great," said McCabe with obvious false bonhomie. "I'm just happy this is working out for all of us."

The good-naturedness was so transparently insincere that Frank felt an ominous note of foreboding as he put down the phone.

"That's him," Frank said to Matt.

"He sounds sort of . . ." Matt shrugged and rolled his eyes. "Weird."

"That's about the size of it, Matt," said Frank Connor, smiling as he ruffled his son's hair. "That just about sums it up."

It did not take long for the plan to begin to unravel, but Frank Connor was unprepared for the quarter the trouble came from. All along he had been expecting McCabe to mess up the deal, to make another set of demands, to become more and more unreasonable, using the pain and suffering of an innocent child to stretch and finally break Frank Connor.

But that did not happen. Rather, the whole plan was shot down in a moment, the bad news given to him by his friend and superior, Jeremiah Cassidy.

Late the next morning Cassidy summoned Frank to his office and sat him down facing him across his desk.

"I checked with the warden up in Pelican Bay, Frank," Cassidy said. "And he said no. Turned me down flat." He shrugged. "I'm sorry."

"He *what*?" Frank shook his head quickly, like a

boxer shaking off a crunching blow to the jaw. ''The warden said *what?*''

''I told you. He said no.''

''Jesus.'' The hope drained out of him. ''What about the governor? Did you ask the governor? What did he say?''

''*He* didn't say anything,'' said Cassidy. ''His office said he did not have time to hear the case.''

''Not enough time?'' Frank couldn't believe what he was hearing. It was *Matt* who didn't have enough time. Not some hack politician in Sacramento.

''That's what they said, Frank.''

''I don't believe it.''

Cassidy leaned forward in his desk chair and lowered his voice as if the governor or one of his minions could hear him.

''Read between the lines, Frank. California has become a law and order state. No politician wants to be accused of coddling criminals. Particularly a psycho like McCabe stuck in Pelican Bay.''

''But what about Matt?''

''They said no, Frank. They said they didn't have time.''

''I need five minutes,'' said Connor desperately. ''He's here in town, today. He must have five minutes. On an elevator, in a car, on the way to the airport. Anywhere, anytime.''

A note of command crept into Cassidy's voice. ''They said no.''

Frank hung his head for a moment, then looked around Cassidy's office as if something there might make sense of this revolting development.

And, in an odd way, there was. The walls of Cassidy's office were not decorated with pictures of his family and with certificates of citation, the honors that police captains tended to pick up in the course of their careers.

Instead, in this series of photographs, there were pictures of Cassidy shaking hands with celebrities and politicians. There were photos of him with the last three governors of California, as well as three of five living presidents. One wall was devoted to pictures of Cassidy with some famous actors and actresses who had made movies in San Francisco, the films helped along with the assistance and cooperation of the SFPD.

Suddenly Frank realized that Cassidy had gotten where he was by playing it smart—and that he wasn't going to stop his steady rise by doing otherwise. He hated himself for even thinking it, but suddenly Frank Connor was wondering how much his friend had pushed for his son, or had he been careful not to push too hard for fear of besmirching his own career?

Had he asked at all?

chapter 4

Governor Tom Morris hated surprises. He liked things to be on time and on schedule, meticulously following the punctilious timetable worked out by his chief of staff Sarah Davis.

Her appointment had been something of a surprise to state house watchers. Morris had always relied on old-fashioned, trench warfare political operatives, but he had gotten rid of the old team at the beginning of his second term and brought in Davis and, so far, things were working out. Morris was a shoo-in for another term—so the early polls said—unless, of course, he had ambitions toward higher office. The polls suggested that this was not out of the question either.

Sarah Davis was thought to be part of this plan. Perhaps because she was a young, attractive woman, she thought she had to work harder and faster than anybody else. Perhaps she felt she needed to be more ruthless than the most hardened political staffer to prove that she could play with the big boys. Closer to the truth, though, was the fact that her pretty, blond exterior hid the implacability of the toughest political animal, a trait she seemed to have been born with, rather than having developed it to fly in the face of conventional political wisdom.

Governor Morris was just finishing up his address to the Commonwealth Club—it was not the first time he had spoken to this eminent group of San Franciscans—and Sarah was parked in the wings of the stage looking over the schedule she already knew by heart. She also knew the speech by heart, but that didn't stop her from listening to it for the tenth or twentieth time.

The governor was just going into his windup, he was in the home stretch, and Sarah was already, in her mind, well on to the next event.

". . . and inspired by your trust and armed with your generous support . . ."

There was a certain amount of laughter on that line. Sarah frowned when she heard it. Were they laughing at him or with him? It made a difference.

". . . we'll win this election and get the state back on its feet."

The audience applauded enthusiastically—they were laughing with him—as Governor Morris beamed, waved, and was discreetly ushered from the stage by Sarah.

The first thing she did was consult her watch, shaking her head, amazed at the accuracy of his delivery. He never failed to deliver his speeches on time.

''How do you do that?'' Sarah asked, laughing. ''You're Mr. Right-On-Time?''

Governor Morris grinned as if she had cracked a dirty joke. ''Practice,'' he said. ''Now what's next?''

''You fly to San Diego, kick butt with some nice, golf-playing, white Republicans,'' said Sarah. She didn't even have to look at her notes. ''Then beer and chowder up in La Jolla where you—''

Suddenly the room was bathed in the bright glow of camera lights.

''Governor Morris . . .''

Instinctively, like the needle on a compass, Governor Morris turned toward the camera. It was hard to tell if he was smiling because he had caught sight of a pretty woman or because he was unable to resist a television camera. He realized too late that he was being ambushed by Dawn Yoshioka and a television crew.

''Dawn Yoshioka,'' said Morris, quickly going into his glad-handing mode. ''Hey, it's nice to see you again, Dawn—''

Dawn was not in the mood to be glad-handed. She grabbed Frank Connor by the arm and pushed him toward Morris.

''Governor, this is Inspector Frank Connor of the San Francisco Police Department,'' she said. Frank looked faintly embarrassed to be the center of attention, but this had to be done.

''Nice to meet you, Frank,'' said the governor, putting out his hand but beginning to look faintly puzzled by the sudden appearance of the press and a cop. ''Always happy to meet one of San Francisco's finest.''

''You remember our appeal when Frank's son was trying to find a donor for a bone marrow transplant? We've done a number of broadcasts on it.''

Governor Morris had no idea what she was talking about, but he covered his ignorance well. ''Of course I remember, Dawn.'' He turned to Connor. ''How is your boy, Frank? Did you find a donor for him?''

''Yes, sir,'' Frank replied quickly. ''He's Peter McCabe.''

''Peter McCabe,'' Governor Morris said, as if the name should mean something to him.

It rang a bell with Sarah Davis too. ''McCabe? Peter McCabe? Why do I know that name?''

''He's in maximum security at Pelican Bay,'' said Frank. ''Life without possibility of parole.''

''Oh, for God's sake,'' said Sarah Davis. She saw exactly where this was going and it was not a position she wanted the governor in. But she knew the camera was rolling and there was nothing she and the governor could do but roll with it.

''The transplant can't be performed at the prison,'' said Frank quickly. ''And the warden will only let him be moved out on your authority.''

The instant she heard that, Sarah's built-in political land-mine alarm went off. She made sure she was well off camera before she waved her arms, as if signaling a missed field goal, silently mouthing ''No fucking way,'' as she did so.

''What do you say, Governor?'' said Dawn. ''Will you help Matt Connor?''

The governor glanced at Frank, at Dawn, and then at the video camera, its red light blinking. He knew when he had been set up and, from a professional point of view, he had to admit that Dawn Yoshioka and this cop had done a pretty good job. They had him cold, well and truly nailed. It was either say yes and hope that a callous criminal behaved himself or else it was: *Governor refuses to help dying child—film at eleven. . . .*

He smiled sardonically to himself, then flashed a big grin for public consumption. "Hey, I've got kids of my own, Frank. What alternative is there?"

Peter McCabe was halfway through John Henry Abbot's famous memoir of prison life, *In the Belly of the Beast*—he had read it before, it was his favorite light reading—when the door of his cage rattled; a guard was rapping on the food slot to get his attention.

"McCabe." The disembodied voice on the other side of the door was gruff. "You have to sign for these things."

McCabe checked the food slot and found a manila envelope, a cup of coffee, four packs of sugar, and a dun-colored prison form.

The guard waited as McCabe set the coffee and sugar on a ledge and dumped the contents of the envelope on his bed: two packs of cigarettes and a disposable lighter. McCabe shook one out, lit it, and inhaled deeply. He looked over at the guard.

"These smokes are stale," McCabe grumbled. "You tell that cop and his dead kid that I ain't gonna stand for stale cigarettes."

"Just sign the form."

McCabe signed the form and slid it back through the slot in the door. He grabbed the four packs of sugar, tore off the tops, and dumped them in the tepid coffee, then sat on the bed with his smoke and his coffee waiting until he heard the guard's footsteps receding.

When he was satisfied that the guard was gone, McCabe put down his coffee and placed his right thumb on the metal edge of the bed, breathed deep, as if mustering his courage, then slammed his thumb as hard as he could with the heel of his left hand. The ball joint at the base of his thumb popped right out of its socket. Then, quickly, he popped his thumb back into the socket.

The pain was intense and McCabe doubled over, his mouth open in a silent scream. He stamped his feet and thrashed from side to side in an attempt to master the agony.

After a minute or two, the fire in his hand began to subside. McCabe went back to his coffee and cigarette with a small smile playing on his lips.

chapter 5

There was a quiet, rather studious air about Frank Connor's partner, Nate Oliver. It was hard to imagine that he had started out in the SFPD like everyone else, in a patrol car, working the tougher streets of the city, busting junkies and drug dealers, being the first uniform on a crime scene. He had done his job on the street well, staying low-key, never losing his temper, keeping an even keel, never straying into the role of bullying street intimidator, but never identified as a pushover either.

His move up the ladder of the department had been swift and sure and his position in the Detective division suited him. He had been assigned to Frank Connor and, despite the fact they had no history together, they had gotten on well and had worked together as an efficient unit. They had become friends.

As the tragedy of Matt's illness deepened and Frank Connor found himself more and more preoccupied with doctors, specialists, hospitals, and, of course, the media, Nate Oliver took up the slack on the police side of things. He quietly did far more than his fair share of the case work assigned to the two men, realizing that Frank Connor had other, more pressing things on his mind. It was his way of helping out in a difficult situation and he didn't mind carrying the extra workload.

While the course and curing of Matt's illness had become paramount in Frank Connor's mind, he found that Matt's plight brought with it a series of smaller details that bedeviled him. The treatment of myelogenous leukemia was a very expensive undertaking. The medications, the continuous hospital stay, the twenty-four-hour nursing, the extensive chemotherapy had added up to a vast figure, an amount of money that had completely wiped out his police department insurance and the loan he had taken from the San Francisco Police Officers Credit Union.

All Connor had left now was his salary, and in order to stretch it to cover the basics of Matt's treatment, Frank had let other bills go. He was behind on all of his credit cards and he was just managing to pay the mortgage on the apartment he shared with Matt in the Sunset District of the city.

Collection agencies were relentless, calling him at all hours of the day or night. They had discovered that he did not spend much time at home—though every night when he returned to his house, he found his answering machine jammed with "extremely important" messages from bill collectors working for Visa, MasterCard, and American Express—so Frank found himself harassed mercilessly at work. Only Samantha Hawkins had not presented a bill for her services and Frank Connor was grateful for that. If he ever got hold of any money, hers would be the account he would settle first.

Frank and Nate had desks facing one another on the third floor of police headquarters. Nate was studying a set of architectural plans at his desk as he studiously avoided listening to Frank as he battled with yet another bill collector.

"Look," said Frank a little desperately, "I'm really sorry. . . . I know I said I'd make the payment on the first but . . . I'll get the payment to you, I swear. Just give me a few more days, a week. . . . A week. Thank you. Thank you very much."

When Frank hung up, sweat had gathered on his brow and he shuddered with embarrassment and loathing. He hated being a deadbeat, but he could not help it, not this time.

It wasn't as though he was *squandering* his money on fripperies; every penny he could shake loose went to Matt. That's just the way it was going to have to be and if he ruined his credit in the course of it, that could not be helped. If that was the worst casualty that came out of this whole, horrible affair, Frank Connor could live with it.

Nate's eyes had not left the plans spread out before him. "Listen to me," Nate began. "There's a way out of your money problems, you know. . . ."

Frank knew what was coming. Three collections had already been taken up throughout the police department, from patrolmen on the beat through to the commissioner, the proceeds going to Matt's treatment. It was touching—and needed—but it was also slightly humiliating, though the only person on the force who looked askance at his accepting the charity was Frank Connor himself.

"Nate, please. I can't accept any more from you guys. You know I can't begin to pay back what you've given me already, so—"

Nate took his eyes off the plans and glanced at his partner. "We're not asking you to pay it back, Frank. If it was somebody else's kid you'd be first in line with the money and you wouldn't expect to ever see a dime of it again, would you?"

"Nate, please." Frank Connor twisted in embarrassment. "Let it go, okay?"

But Nate was not to be deterred so easily. "All we're saying—"

"Drop it, okay?" said Frank.

Nate shrugged, his eyes flicking back down to the plans.

"Whatever you say, Frank."

Frank hoped he had not hurt Nate's feelings. "Look, I appreciate the offer."

"Uh-huh," Nate replied. He continued to study the blueprints spread out in front of him. Frank got up from his desk and looked over his partner's shoulder. Nate was examining the layout of San Francisco Memorial Hospital, a complex series of schematics. The building comprised two distinct parts. The old hospital, built after the devastating earthquake of 1906, was a vast, fortresslike building with walls several feet thick, designed to withstand almost any natural disaster.

Adjacent to the old building was a newer, taller,

steel-and-glass tower, a modern structure that incorporated all the antiearthquake technology that had been developed in the ninety years since the last great quake. When San Francisco was hit by an earthquake in 1989 neither the old building nor the new had done more than shake a little.

The two buildings were joined by a steel-and-glass air bridge that connected the top floor of the old building with the fifth floor of the new.

Nate had gotten hold of the plans of the buildings and had been going over every inch, like a general studying a battlefield, looking for any weakness in the layout that Peter McCabe might seize and exploit.

Nate pointed out a series of lines running the length of the buildings. "That's the ventilation system there," he said. "There's a lot of it."

"What are the dimensions of the ducts?" Frank Connor asked.

Nate looked to the key in the lower left-hand corner. "Six by eight inches."

"Too small."

"And a straight drop," Nate noted. "Even if he got into one of those shafts he'd fall at least five stories into the air extraction machinery in the basement." Nate shrugged. "So unless he's immortal, I don't think we have to worry about that aspect of the thing."

The two men were still bent over the plans when Cassidy walked into the office. One look at his face told Nate and Frank that their boss was not in a good mood. His face was dark with anger.

They both knew why he was in such ill humor, of course. ''Oh, shit,'' Nate whispered as Cassidy slammed the door.

Cassidy crossed his arms over his chest and stared at Frank Connor for a moment or two. ''The governor, Connor? You set up the fucking governor with that TV babe? You think guys like him forget that shit? You think guys like me do?''

''Captain, I—''

''You went over my head,'' said Cassidy angrily. ''You know how that makes me look? You have any idea what they're saying up the line?''

The pressures building in Frank could not stay contained forever. Now they blew, in a great fireball of anger that seemed to push Cassidy back physically. Connor jumped to his feet.

''You mean the governor doesn't have time to see me, so my son dies. And I'm supposed to accept that because it's police protocol?'' Connor's voice was echoing down the hallway of the building, broadcasting his frustration and anger for the entire department to hear.

''Frank,'' said Nate softly. ''Calm down. Please. Just sit down and take a deep breath.''

But Frank Connor refused to be calmed down. ''Do you have any idea how much time I took from that kid and gave to this department? Matt came second in my life every day of his life until his mother died. Now things have changed. I'm paying him back!''

Nate was on his feet now, ready to get between Frank and Cassidy. It looked, for a moment, like

Frank was ready to hit his superior officer.

In contrast to Frank, Cassidy kept his voice calm, and his words sounded all the more scary when delivered with such composure.

"I went to bat for you and you fucked me, Frank," Cassidy almost whispered. "I got you in to see McCabe, I went out on the line with the governor and you don't care. You don't care about the governor or me or anybody except Matt, do you?"

Frank's anger died down as quickly as it had flared up. "Sir, I did not want any of this to get on you. I'm truly sorry about that." Frank breathed deep. "But basically, you are right. I don't care about anything else but my son."

Cassidy respected the candor of this and he could not fault the unassailable logic. He was sympathetic, but his anger still showed.

"Well," said Cassidy, thrusting his hands into his pockets. "Shit rolls downhill as usual. The governor barked at the mayor, the mayor reamed the chief, and the chief made me head of the security detail when McCabe comes in for the transplant." He paused a moment to let the words sink in, to give Nate and Frank time to appreciate what a nightmare that assignment would be.

"When this is over, Connor, and Matt's all better, you and I are gonna have a reckoning to do."

Frank nodded. "Thank you, sir." They both knew what the thanks were for. Frank was showing his gratitude that Cassidy was putting all the bad blood aside until this was all over. There would be no retribution, no recriminations until Matt was well and

McCabe was safely returned to his cell in Pelican Bay.

Cassidy glanced over at Nate's desk. "So what is all this shit, Nate?"

"I was just showing Frank the plans for my new cabin." Nate started to roll up the plans quickly. "You know I have a piece of land up in Healdsburg and—"

Cassidy didn't buy this story for a moment. He stopped Nate from rolling up the plans, and forced the sheaves of paper back down on the desk. "Well, well. It looks like your cabin is gonna have a huge hospital, complete with a prison ward, no less."

Cassidy looked to Nate and Frank, then back down at the architectural blueprints. "These are the schematics for San Francisco Memorial Hospital . . . even the plans of the old building." Cassidy sounded slightly impressed. "How come? Talk to me, gentlemen."

It was cards-on-the-table time for Frank and Nate. "Captain— Cop to cop? . . ."

"Cop to cop, Frank," said Cassidy.

"We know McCabe doesn't care about my son," said Connor briskly. "We know that he's got to be planning to escape. That's why he's agreeing to do this."

Cassidy nodded. "Yeah? . . ."

"Father to father?" said Frank.

"What?"

"Let him think it might work," said Frank Connor. "Make him have a reason to come."

Cassidy nodded slightly and allowed himself a tight little smile. "As long as he only *thinks* it's going to work, Frank. That's all."

Frank Connor never left the hospital until Matt had fallen asleep. They sat together, not doing much of anything, not even talking all that much, just passing the time until Matt drifted off.

Sometimes it took a while for him to fall asleep, despite the rigorous regimen of tests and drugs he went through in the course of each day. The natural energy of a nine-year-old, though, was a difficult force to tame. He lay in bed twisting a handful of plastic tubing into complex shapes.

Frank sat by the bed reading the green section of the *San Francisco Chronicle*.

"Dad?"

"Hmmmm? Yeah?" Frank was not paying all that much attention.

"When you have sexual relations with a woman . . . ," Matt began.

Frank dropped the paper and looked at his son. Matt had his attention now—and Frank was doing his best to conceal his astonishment.

Matt seemed a little shy about the matter, but was determined to get the question out. "Do you pee inside her or is it something else?"

"Why are you asking that?" said Frank. "Did some kid say something?"

Matt shrugged. "You know. . . ."

"Who was it?"

"I don't know," said Matt. "So what is it, that stuff?"

"It's not pee," said Frank. "It's something else."

Matt nodded to himself, as if something had been confirmed. "I thought so." He went back to his elaborate construction with the plastic tubing, but it took a moment for Frank to go back to his paper. The instant he did, though, Matt sprung another unexpected question on him.

"Dad?"

"Yeah?"

"Why did they put him in prison?" Matt asked. "Peter. Did he kill people?"

"McCabe," Frank corrected. Using McCabe's first name was uncomfortably personal. It made the criminal into a real person.

"McCabe. . . . He's going to be inside of me, Dad," said Matt. There was real concern in his eyes. "He's going to become part of me."

Frank shook his head vigorously. "Definitely not. Not him. His marrow, his blood cells. . . . But the souls make the mind and the soul is yours. If you get the blood of an old person that doesn't make you old. If you get *my* blood, it wouldn't make you me. You're you and you always will be." Frank leaned closer to his son and looked him straight in the eyes. "You know what I'm saying, Matt?"

Matt nodded, but did not look like he had been reassured all that much.

"If we could pick and choose, kiddo, maybe we'd take somebody else, but . . ." He shrugged and opened his hands as if they had no choice.

"I know," said Matt. "I understand." Matt smiled as Frank reached out and touched his hand. They were at ease with each other, father and son, relaxed and happy that the storm had almost passed.

chapter 6

Peter McCabe stood in the bright light of day, feeling the warm sun on his face for the first time in many months. He put a cigarette in his mouth and lit it with the lighter he had been given and inhaled deeply, enjoying the simple pleasures of a cigarette, the sun, and some fresh air. For a moment he could forget that he was in the Pelican Bay "shoe"—the shoebox-sized exercise yard.

A basketball game was going on at one end of the yard and the rest of the prisoners sitting here and there pretended to watch the game, but stole quick, stealthy glances at McCabe as he ambled across the yard. Everyone knew about him—none had actually met him—for his reputation as the hardest case in the hardest prison in the country had preceded him. No one chose to meet his eye, as if there were some voodoo power in McCabe's gaze, a look that could kill a man.

On the far side of the yard, sitting on a bench with another inmate, was the man Peter McCabe was anxious to meet, a grizzled lifer named Sturgiss, rumored to be Pelican Bay's most reliable drug connection.

As McCabe ambled toward the bench, Sturgiss's seatmate saw him coming and stood up. ''Incoming,'' he whispered and walked away.

Sturgiss didn't move when McCabe sat down next to him, sitting close—too close—to the old prisoner. Neither man looked at the other; both of them pretended to focus on the basketball game. There was one standout player, a young, lithe black man, who slipped through defenders like a snake. Every time he went to the basket he scored.

''That kid's got nice moves,'' McCabe observed. ''Know his name?'' He did not see Sturgiss wince when he asked about the young man, but he knew he did. ''Maybe you could introduce me to him.''

''I know who you are, McCabe,'' Sturgiss growled. ''And I can't get you no drugs, okay?''

''Drugs?'' said McCabe, looking genuinely nonplussed by the suggestion. ''I hate drugs. Drugs are nothing more than voluntary enslavement. A modern plague, that's what drugs are.''

''That's good. Because I can't get you none.'' Sturgiss shifted uneasily, wondering what McCabe's game was. It was a *sure* thing that he was up to something. Inmates like McCabe always had some scheme going.

''No, no drugs for me,'' said McCabe easily. ''What you can get me is an antidrug. Narcan. Four milligrams in a vial. It's a counteractive, used for overdose cases. There's this kid I gotta save, see. And I need the Narcan, Sturgiss."

"I heard about that kid," Sturgiss replied. His eyes did not leave the basketball game. "And I know all about Narcan. . . . Narcan isn't going to do a damn thing for him, either."

Narcan was the brand name of the generic drug named naloxone, a miracle medication that seemed to inhibit and eliminate any narcotic in the bloodstream. It was effective on all kinds of drugs, even things as potent as heroin. Sturgiss couldn't understand for a moment why it would be of interest to Peter McCabe.

Sturgiss stood to go, but McCabe reached up and grabbed him by the shoulder, squeezing hard, jamming his thumb into the pressure point above the shoulder blade. Sturgiss felt the numbing pain in his arm and sat down again, struggling to show no distress.

"Forget it, McCabe," said Sturgiss. He thought he knew why McCabe had hurt him—to prove that it wouldn't take much for him to kill him. He was not scared. "I've been in lockup half my life. The worst you can do to me is kill me—and you'd be doing me a favor. I don't care about me, I don't care about you, and I don't care about no fucking kid with cancer."

McCabe shook his head slowly, as if surprised that people could misread his intentions so egregiously. He slumped back on the bench and narrowed his eyes, watching the game with a special intensity.

"You miss the point, Sturgiss," he said. "I'm not talking about our cancer kid. I'm talking about our

Scottie Pippen here." He gestured idly toward the basketball game, not pointing out anyone in particular, but making it plain who he was talking about. "Talking about saving *his* life. Understand?"

McCabe now had Sturgiss's undivided attention. He chanced a quick look at McCabe.

"His name is Jonathan Booth," McCabe continued, "and he's in here for whacking some cop while high on PCP. Lots of courage when he was screwed up. . . . The instant he comes down he's a pushover. . . . I hear he's one scared puppy when he doesn't get his morphine. But you keep him fixed up, don't you, old man?"

Sturgiss did not dare to move. He scarcely dared to breathe. If McCabe had found out this much about him and Booth then he knew the whole story. . . .

"You call him Johnnyboo when you're sweating on top of him, thinking about your wife, that lovely woman you clubbed to death twenty-six years ago . . . or was it thirty-six?" McCabe shrugged. "I guess it doesn't matter, does it? It was a while ago."

Sturgiss and McCabe watched Jonathan on the court, the young man blissfully unaware that his future, his life, was being discussed so coldly.

McCabe turned philosophical. "Love is an odd bird, isn't it? You don't care about your own life, but Johnnyboo's death would cost you great pain, wouldn't it, old man?"

Sturgiss sat absolutely still, as if he feared that McCabe was a snake about to strike.

"So I will kill your strange son, and I shall do it in a terrible and disfiguring fashion. Unless"—he turned to Sturgiss and smiled—"unless you put a vial of Narcan in my hand tomorrow. You will do that and you will tell nobody about it. Because . . . well, old and useless as you are, you do care. And that is a good thing.''

McCabe stood up and tapped Sturgiss on the shoulder—inflicting no pain this time—then he walked away, flexing his thumb in and out of its socket as he went. Sturgiss watched him go, then he looked over at the kid on the basketball court. A lump came to his throat as he watched the man he loved.

The hospital was getting ready for Peter McCabe. Joe Marquez was Cassidy's point man at the hospital and it fell to the crew-cutted ex-military man to show what had been done to make sure that everything was secure and that the transplant went smoothly. At the last minute, Sarah Davis had gotten involved, sent down to San Francisco by Governor Morris to make sure that nothing went wrong with this particular political hot potato. There was the chance, if this all worked out, that the governor could make some political hay out of it. Sarah was attuned to all possibilities.

''The boy will stay in a separate room at all times,'' said Marquez, pointing to an operating room off the corridor. ''McCabe will enter through Emergency in a security chair, then come up here.''

''Where the press can be—'' Sarah stated.

''Nowhere near him,'' finished Cassidy.

''You sure about that?'' Sarah Davis asked. ''The governor wondered if—''

''Ms. Davis,'' said Cassidy, ''we are dealing with

a very dangerous man here. We want to keep people away from him, not get cozy.''

Marquez led the way into the operating room. The small group stood in the middle of the sterile chamber looking around. There was a glassed-in gallery overlooking the operating room. Sarah wondered if at least *that* could be turned over to the press. She made a note to ask Cassidy later.

''McCabe will be wheeled in from the pre-op side,'' said Marquez. ''Then prepped. Then fully sedated. He will be unconscious throughout the procedure and, I believe, shackled at all times.'' He looked over to Cassidy. ''Is that correct?''

Cassidy shook his head. ''No,'' he said firmly. ''Not shackles. Leather straps. You can't pick the lock on a leather strap.''

This remark generated a certain amount of amusement among the listeners, but neither Cassidy nor Frank Connor saw anything funny in it. As the party moved on, Frank hung back, scanning the room for dangers, both visible and hidden.

''Well,'' said Marquez. ''In any case, even if he were to get free, there are no exits he could possibly take out of here.''

Cassidy and Frank Connor exchanged looks. Both of them hated overconfidence—particularly where Peter McCabe was concerned.

The Pelican Bay prison library was a dreary, windowless room, its cinderblock walls painted the usual, uniform government green. The few low shelves held a collection of law books, as well as dog-eared volumes donated by Prisoners' Aid and other do-good agencies. There were a couple of old, slow computers. McCabe sat at one, peering at the screen, carefully reading an article from an Encarta CD on turn-of-the-century building techniques. The article focused on the life and career of a California architect named J. C. Reynolds, a major figure in the rebuilding of the city of San Francisco after the 1906 earthquake.

The plans on his screen were nothing like as detailed as the schemes Nate and Frank had been studying, but McCabe had picked up some interesting information. He had learned how public buildings erected after the 1906 earthquake had been powered (partially by electricity) and that they all received city-supplied steam.

As a guard approached, McCabe picked up a disk from the table and jammed it into the A drive of the machine and hit a key hard. But the building plans and layouts stayed on his screen as the old, slow drive tried to figure out which command to follow and in what order. Quickly, but without panicking—McCabe ejected the disk and reloaded. Just as the guard arrived the plans vanished, giving way to a computer-generated chessboard.

"Who's winning?" the CO asked.

"These computer chess programs are too easy," said McCabe boastfully. "Bring me Garry Kasparov. Hell, bring me Deep Thought."

McCabe could be charming when he wanted to be, even suckering this guard into a joke.

"Finish up. Lunch in twenty."

As the guard walked away, McCabe hot-keyed the computer and the information on Reynolds scrolled back onto the screen. He read as fast as he could to finish before the guard returned and evicted him from the library.

Back at the hospital, the tour of the secure facilities was progressing. Marquez had led the visitors across the bridge connecting the new hospital building with the old structure. The interior of the 1907 building was different, a trifle run-down. Whereas in the new building all of the infrastructure was hidden, the ceilings and walls of the old building were crisscrossed with heating, water, and electrical pipes that snaked along corridors and down stairwells.

"Don't let the age of the old place fool you," said Marquez, his voice full of pride. "Our security hardware is state of the art."

Marquez led them down the corridor. Ahead were two gates, sliding steel barriers that crossed the hallway at points about thirty feet apart. Standing at the first set of gates was a heavyset man in his forties.

"This is Ed Fayne," said Marquez. "He's the prison warden. He'll take it from here. The hospital ward is his baby."

There did seem to be a bit of house pride about Fayne. "The old building has walls of concrete two feet thick. And there's an inch of rolled steel over every entrance—the whole place is computer controlled. We can lock the whole building down in seconds."

He led his group of visitors through the gates and into the security booth, the guardhouse that controlled the whole prison ward complex. Two deputies were stationed there, both of them watching the bank of video monitors set in control panels.

"Every square centimeter is monitored," Fayne continued, as the visitors crowded around the monitors, looking at the prison ward from a dozen different angles.

"We see trouble—" Fayne stuck out a meaty thumb and punched a red button. The television screens showed the views from all over the ward as doors slammed shut, gates dropped, bars dropped into place.

"In twenty minutes we'll have this bad boy shut up tighter than a fish's asshole." He laughed at his own joke. Frank wondered how many times he had cracked it over the years.

Fayne grinned and winked at Sarah Davis. Well-dressed, pretty women were something of a rarity on a prison ward.

Sarah grinned back, but rather because she was cheered by the sight of all this security than she was by the sight of Ed Fayne, whom she considered something of a toad. She turned to Frank.

"See," she said happily, "there seems to be nothing to worry about."

"Right," he said.

But Frank was not grinning. He was studying the computer system, watching the monitors showing alternative views of the prison inside and out. It looked like a morass of shifting possibilities, too complex to control.

chapter 7

The drug cart moved down the tiers of the general population cell block, part of a little procession: Sturgiss, the cart, and two guards handing out drugs to the prisoners. Most of the medications they handed out were antidepressants, handfuls of Paxil, Zoloft, and Prozac went down the throats of murderers and rapists as if they were so many neurotic baby boomers. More serious cases got jolting doses of chlopromazine and lithium.

And although McCabe was antidrug, he was required to take the minimum dose of Prozac—the prison authorities feared depression in a group of men with every reason to be depressed—an invasion of his body and an abridgment of his rights he had always resented, but today he was glad of it.

The medicine cart came to a halt in front of his cell and the guard handed McCabe his dose and a paper cup of water. McCabe didn't take it immediately though. Rather, he stared the guard in the eye, intimidating the man silently, until he looked away. Then McCabe threw back his head and swallowed—as he did so, he felt the slightest touch on the breast pocket of his jumpsuit. Sturgiss had made his delivery.

The drug cart moved on and McCabe stepped back into his cell. His back to the door, he slid the vial of Narcan out of his pocket and pulled a length of dental floss from its dispenser. Working quickly, McCabe tied one end of the dental floss around the slim tube and made a slipknot on the other end. He opened his mouth as wide as he could and managed to slip the loose knot around a rear molar, then lowered the ampule of Narcan down his throat. It was awkward, the waxy string lying in his esophagus like something to be coughed up, but it was bearable. Quickly, he pulled the glass tube out of his gullet, wrapped the floss around it, and hid it under the mattress of his bunk.

Next, McCabe grabbed his disposable lighter and popped the top off. He removed the flint and hid it under the long nail he had been cultivating on his right thumb. In a quick test he scraped his thumb against the cinderblock wall and was rewarded with a bright orange flash of spark.

"Good," said McCabe. It was plain that he was very pleased with himself. "I'm ready."

Later that day Cassidy, accompanied by one of his officers, a man called Colton, arrived at Pelican Bay to be the official representatives of the San Francisco Police Department in the little convoy that would transport Peter McCabe from prison to the hospital in the city.

They got their first look at McCabe through the window of the prison sick bay. He was shackled to the security chair, of course, but dressed in a surgical gown, his right leg straight out on an operating table. A prison doctor had opened a small incision in McCabe's thigh and was inserting a tiny transmitter under the skin. McCabe appeared to be undergoing the short procedure without any anesthesia, yet scarcely flinching as the doctor put a stitch in the leg to close the wound.

In the observation room a technician turned on a receiver, checking the coordinates of the transmitter as the little device came to life.

"What's the accuracy on that thing?" Colton asked Cassidy.

"We'll know where he is to within twenty feet," Cassidy replied.

"And the range is over twenty-five miles," said the technician, handing the receiver to Cassidy. "Anything over that and he's outrun you."

"If he gets twenty-five miles away from us we're already in big trouble," said Cassidy grimly. "I don't want him out of our sight."

The guards in the prison sick bay were locking special shackles onto McCabe's ankles.

"Hey," said McCabe almost gleefully. "Reinforced tungsten steel. It would take an acetylene torch twenty minutes or more to cut through them. Trust me." He sounded honored that such expensive precautions were being taken to make sure he would not escape.

"What are you so cheerful about?" asked one of the guards.

"Why not?" McCabe replied, a wide grin on his face. "I'm gonna go on a trip. See San Francisco. It's my favorite city." He looked through the window, smiling straight at Cassidy. Cassidy did not return the smile.

It took another twenty-five minutes to load McCabe into the armored van that would carry him to the city. He was shackled hand and foot, with a body chain around his waist, then locked into a security chair that had been bolted to the floor of the truck. Three guards climbed in with him and the door locked from the outside.

Then, flanked by two patrol cars, a Department of Corrections helicopter chattering overhead, the convoy slowly made its way through the gates of the prison, then down Highway 101 toward San Francisco.

San Francisco Memorial Hospital was a hive of activity as well, getting ready for the arrival of the notorious Peter McCabe. Sarah Davis had been all over the place arranging the print and electronic media, hoping for the most exposure.

Frank and the rest of the cops on the scene were a little unhappy with the abundance of press—anything or anyone who might get in the way was a threat to security. Frank was ninety-nine percent sure that McCabe was going to try something and he wanted to be in a position to stop any break he might make dead in its tracks.

A crowd of reporters milling around did not make

that any easier. Frank was standing with Nate when Sarah Davis came up to him, breathless and excited.

"We've got live feeds from three stations," she announced. "And reporters from the print media from as far away as L.A. and San Diego."

"Great," said Frank, his voice hollow.

"They want a statement from you, Frank," said Sarah. "And they're going to want at least a photo-op with Matt at some point."

Frank Connor glanced at his watch. "Sorry," he said. "Now, I've got to—"

Sarah looked at him critically. "A word to the wise, Frank. You used the governor. Now you owe him. You know what I'm saying?"

Frank glanced at Nate, who nodded. "The lady has a point, Frank."

"Damn right I do," said Davis.

"I'll give you a statement and I'll specifically thank the governor when the procedure has been successfully completed, okay? As for any pictures of Matt—that's up to his doctors."

Sarah Davis grimaced. She did not look happy at all. "That's not much of a deal, Frank, considering what's on the line here."

"Would you like me to publicly endorse him for reelection?" said Frank evenly.

Sarah smiled dryly. "I think that would be a little obvious, don't you?"

"You're the expert," said Frank. "Now I do have to get to my son. . . ."

The radiation room was on the ninth floor of the new building, a white, sterile space completely dominated by the vast bulk of a sixty-cobalt radiation linear accelerator that would deliver total body radiation. It was a submarinelike tube, like an MRI scanner, which Matt would be slid into for a heavy dose of radiation.

He was already in his hospital gown when Nate and Frank made it up to the room. Nate had never seen the RLA before and he gulped when he saw the daunting device now. He and Frank, along with Dr. Hawkins, were supposed to be there to buck up the boy, but Matt looked calmer than all three adults. Still, Nate did his best. "Listen, Matt, when you get the module landed on the asteroid, I want you to call in, okay?"

Matt went along with the game, but he was doing it more for Nate's sake than his own. "We'll have to maintain radio silence, Captain, or the Borgs are sure to lock on to our signal."

"You know, I hadn't thought of that." Nate could sense Matt's detachment and he glanced over at Frank. He was watching his son with quiet respect.

"Okay," said Dr. Hawkins briskly. "Matt, do you know what this machine is called?"

Matt knew all too well what it was and he recited like a schoolboy repeating a boring lesson learned by rote. "It's a radiation linear accelerator," Matt said wearily. "You're going to use it to kill my bone marrow cells so you can replace them with good ones."

Hawkins nodded, impressed at his composure and knowledge. "That's right. Any questions?"

"Just one. . . . Will it hurt?"

The doctor shook her head. "Nope. You won't

feel a thing. Just a little nausea afterward, that's all. Nothing to worry about.''

''Nausea is a thing,'' said Matt unhappily. ''Will I lose my hair again?''

''No,'' said Hawkins. ''You only lose your hair with chemotherapy.''

Throughout his bout with cancer, Matt had been pricked and poked and prodded and he had taken it all in stride. The loss of his hair to chemotherapy had been the one thing that had made Matt upset—until one day his father had hit on a solution.

''If you lose yours this time,'' said Frank. ''I'll shave my head again.''

Matt smiled, remembering the first time he had seen his father's head shaved as smooth as a cue ball. ''That's a deal.''

The kid was so calm that the adults in the room seemed almost to be in awe of him.

''This will take about an hour,'' said Hawkins. ''Maybe we should get started.''

Matt nodded. ''Make it so.'' It was a line from ''Star Trek,'' but it was more than that. As Matt smiled up at Nate and Frank he seemed to be assuring them that despite his calm he was still just a boy after all. As he started to slide into the giant machine, Frank took his son's hand and squeezed it.

''I'm with you.''

Matt smiled and squeezed back. ''I know.'' Then his small body disappeared into the RLA device as if he had been fed to it.

''Someday,'' said Nate quietly, ''I'd like to be just like him.''

''This is going to greatly weaken his immune system,'' said Hawkins. There was a look of real concern on her face. ''Once he gets McCabe's bone marrow, it'll come back, but until then we have to be extremely cautious about opportunistic infection.''

Cassidy did not stay with the convoy transporting Peter McCabe down from Pelican Bay. Once the little procession hit the freeway, Cassidy turned on his lights and siren and drove at code one speed all the way back to the city.

He arrived at the hospital at just about the time Matt went into the RLA, and he swept into the temporary police command post that had been set up next door to the operating room where the marrow extraction would take place.

Marquez was waiting for him.

''We have about an hour,'' said Cassidy.

''Okay,'' said Marquez, leading the way into the command post. There were dozens of phones, radios, monitors, and a dozen heavily armed men to operate them all. Cassidy looked grim but satisfied with what had been done, but Marquez took it another way.

''This is all kind of overkill, isn't it?'' he said, looking slightly bemused.

Cassidy glared at him and thought: *Unreliable. . . .*

The convoy had passed through Oakland and was on the Bay Bridge approaching Treasure Island, the lights of San Francisco illuminating the sky ahead of them.

Those inside the van could see none of that, of

course. His hands behind his back, McCabe had been flexing his injured thumb all the way down from the prison, popping the ball of the joint in and out of the socket for almost three hours. It hardly hurt at all now. The ampule of Narcan was hidden in his throat. He was looking forward to the action.

McCabe smiled at one of the guards. "I love the city," he said affably. "Don't you?"

chapter 8

Matt came out of the radiation linear accelerator feeling woozy and sick to his stomach. He was pale and shaky, the confidence and the composure gone now, as if the machine had squeezed the poise and self-assurance out of him. To Frank he looked like what he was: a frail, scared, desperately ill little boy. When he saw his father, though, a little color came into his cheeks and the bright light of excitement lit up his eyes.

"Dad? Dad?" said Matt, half rising from the gurney. "It's almost over now, isn't it?"

As Frank rushed to his son's side, the radio on his hip crackled to life. "He's coming," some cop's voice said through it. "McCabe is just about to arrive."

Frank snapped off the radio and squeezed his son's shoulder. "I'm here for you, Matt. But I gotta go now. I have to check on McCabe. But you'll be okay with Nate, right?''

''No problem,'' said Nate as Matt nodded and smiled. Frank started to go, then stopped, hesitating. He wanted to stay with his son—let others take care of McCabe—but he had set this in motion and he should be part of it if there was going to be any trouble.

As the convoy pulled in to the forecourt of the hospital, McCabe managed to catch a quick glimpse of the two buildings, the new and the old, connected by the air bridge on the fifth floor. Then the guard closed the slit in the side of the van.

''We're here,'' he said as the van drove into a bay of the hospital garage.

The first thing McCabe saw when the doors of the van swung open were two San Francisco tactical cops in full body armor, both men standing there with huge, snarling German shepherds on short choke chains. Standing next to them was Cassidy.

''Okay,'' Cassidy ordered. ''Get him out.'' The guards got on both sides of the chair and lifted McCabe to the ground.

The tactical cops led their dogs forward to allow them to get McCabe's scent. He stared down at them as their moist snouts sniffed at his trouser cuffs, a look in his eyes suggesting that he was an animal just like them. Then, as if to prove it, McCabe suddenly made a quick hissing noise and the two dogs jumped back in fright, their bushy tails between their legs.

McCabe cackled. Cassidy scowled. "Come on," he growled. "Move it."

They pushed McCabe through the swinging double doors of the emergency room and straight down one of the corridors toward the elevators. McCabe looked around at the bustle and the people as if he was out on a tour. Then he saw Frank moving toward him.

Their eyes met and locked. Both men knew what was coming. McCabe spoke with disturbing casualness. "How's Matt, Frank?"

But before Frank could answer, McCabe was wheeled onto an elevator, a burly uniformed cop getting between Connor and the steel doors.

"No access," said the policeman. "Cassidy's orders."

All nonessential hospital personnel had been moved out of the corridor on the second floor. The only white coat McCabe saw when the elevator doors opened was Samantha Hawkins. McCabe smiled at her as she fell in line with the entourage.

"I'm Dr. Hawkins," she said. "I shall be doing the extraction."

"I'm sorry I cannot greet you properly," McCabe replied.

Despite the restraints, McCabe inclined his head toward her, a little bow of the head. It was a small gesture, but filled with a certain surprising dignity. Hawkins, caught off guard by the little nod, felt compelled to acknowledge it, bowing slightly in return.

"So, you're a pediatric oncologist," said McCabe in a friendly tone of voice, as if he was starting a pleasant conversation with a pretty stranger he had just met at a cocktail party.

"That's right," said Hawkins.

"So when all your friends in med school were settling for cushy specialties in plastic surgery and cardiology, you decided to go the hard route." Peter McCabe smiled and nodded as if admiring her courageous choice of her line of work.

Hawkins smiled again, but was aware of him, sensing not only his intelligence, but the power of his personality as well.

"Where did you go to medical school?" McCabe asked pleasantly.

"Shut the fuck up, McCabe," Cassidy snapped. "No talking."

Hawkins waved away Cassidy's order. "UC San Francisco," she said to McCabe. Then to Cassidy: "We're going to need—"

"You're an attractive woman, Doctor," said McCabe with a little smile. "And your competence especially is very appealing."

Hawkins glanced down at him, momentarily nonplussed by McCabe, then over at the cops. "Do your men know where to go?" she asked Cassidy.

"I'm in there with you," said Cassidy. "Kellen is outside the door on the pre-op side and Trimble is on the post-op side."

Frank Connor, who had raced up the fire stairs, arrived just in time to hear the dispositions of the policemen.

"I'm inside too," said Frank urgently.

Cassidy took him by the arm and pulled him out of earshot of McCabe. "You're too involved here,

Frank,'' he said. Cassidy was not being gruff or difficult. As he spoke, his words were friendly but firm. ''I can't have you in there. You know that.''

''But—''

Cassidy was not going to listen to any objections. ''If Matt was in there too, that would be one thing. But this is just McCabe. You don't have to be there.''

''I think I should be.''

''I think you shouldn't. That's final.''

Hawkins stepped into the argument. ''There is an observation gallery one level up,'' she said. ''You can watch from there. There's no room for you in the OR. Okay, Frank?''

Frank did not like it, but he could tell from the looks on the faces of Cassidy and Hawkins that it was the best he was going to get. As he turned to go, he caught sight of Peter McCabe. He was smiling at him.

There were two operating room nurses, two residents, and an anesthesiologist in the OR, all of them scrubbed up, suited, and waiting. Hawkins appeared a moment later dressed in the same green clothing, just as McCabe was wheeled into the room.

''Get a gown on him,'' she ordered, ''and get him transferred.''

Cassidy stepped up, shaking his head. ''No gown,'' he said. ''Not unless you can put it on without removing the restraints.''

Hawkins pursed her lips and thought for a moment. ''Okay, just get him on the table,'' she said to the two guards.

The men did as they were told, undoing the straps on the security chair. In a moment, McCabe was sitting in the chair with just leg and arm shackles around his waist to restrain him. It was the most free he had been for hours and it felt good.

"Can you stand up and get onto the table?" Hawkins asked.

McCabe nodded and stood, but he couldn't make it onto the operating table. "I can't open my legs wide enough to climb on, Doc," he said.

"Try rolling on," said Cassidy, who got behind him and pushed him up onto the operating table. Once he was spread out on the table, Hawkins leaned over him, trying to see how she could get at the hip. Her face was close to McCabe's and he could smell her perfume, as well as the faint scent of cigarette smoke.

"You're a smoker, Doctor?" McCabe sounded amused and intimate at the same time.

Hawkins was surprised at his perspicacity, but otherwise ignored him. "I cannot get to his hips with the arm shackles on," she said. "I would have to cut through his arms to get there."

"Cassidy would do that for you, Doctor," said McCabe with a chuckle.

"What are the alternatives?" Cassidy asked, speaking across McCabe's body.

"Give him the Demerol right away," said Hawkins. "It'll put him under, then we can consider our options. Dr. Raz?" she said, addressing the anesthesiologist. "Would you prepare the injection, please?"

As Dr. Raz brought over the needle filled with the

anesthetic versed, McCabe's jaws moved slightly as he bit down on the Narcan vial clutched between his teeth. He did not flinch when the needle went into his arm, and a moment after the injection his eyes closed and his body went slack in the shackles.

"Okay," said Hawkins. "Let's get started."

Matt had fallen asleep in his room, but he did not doze for long. He awoke with a start, his throat dry and his stomach churning. Nate was standing over the bed, ever vigilant.

It took a moment for his eyes to focus. "Where's my dad?" Matt asked, his voice dry and croaky.

"He'll be back," said Nate. "How are you feeling?"

"Lousy," said Matt.

"Well, they must have started the extraction by now," said Nate. "It's almost all over, Matt. You'll be good as new in no time."

chapter 9

McCabe appeared to have succumbed almost completely to the narcotic that had been injected into his veins a few minutes before. His arms were secured by leather straps on the operating table and ekg sensors were taped to his arms and scalp. His heart beeped regularly on the monitor, a regular, strong beat.

Dr. Raz held an anesthesia face cup near McCabe's mouth. He placed it over McCabe's face.

"He's breathing normally," the doctor said, glancing over his shoulder. Then he checked the monitors. "The BIS is at seventy."

"Is he out?" Cassidy asked.

Raz nodded. "Another minute and he'll be under completely."

Hawkins selected the extraction needle from the tray of instruments offered by one of the OR nurses. The hypodermic was terrifyingly large—it looked like a bicycle pump with a foot-long needle on the end.

"Is he out now?" Cassidy asked. "He's got to be under now."

Raz frowned at the monitors. "A moment, please. It's not dropping yet. . . ."

No one was paying any attention to McCabe. As the doctors gathered around the ekg and BIS monitors, McCabe popped his thumb out of its socket and squeezed his hand through the cuff around his wrist.

"I don't understand what's going on," said Raz. "He's not responding to anesthesia. But he *looks* like he's unconscious. . . ."

All kinds of alarms went off in Cassidy's skull and he stepped over to McCabe—just in time to see his eyes open.

Suddenly everything seemed to happen at once. McCabe raised his legs and caught Cassidy's neck in the shackle chain and wrapped it tight around him, choking him. McCabe reared up, his free hand stripping off the anesthesia mask, then grabbing Cassidy and throwing him to the floor.

For a second Frank Connor, watching from the observation gallery, was frozen. He realized that something was going wrong, but he took a moment to react. Then he started pounding on the thick glass, screaming for the cops on the door of the operating room.

It was Kellen who realized that something was amiss in the OR. He threw open the door and walked straight into McCabe's first trap.

He had popped the flint out from under his thumbnail and struck it against the metal instrument tray, the single spark igniting the gas escaping from the anesthetic mask. A great gout of flame leaped across the room as McCabe turned the handle on the gas tank, turning the length of tube into a makeshift flamethrower.

As Kellen pounded into the room he got a face full of fire. His hair and flesh burst into flame. He fell back screaming in pain.

Hawkins and the others could only watch as McCabe sat up on the operating table and wrenched his other hand free of the shackles.

He wheeled around with the anesthetic hose, catching Trimble full in the face with a ball of fire as he crashed through the door, his gun drawn. The cop screamed as his entire upper body became engulfed in flame, and he clawed at his face as if trying to rip the fire from his face. As he stumbled blindly, he hit one of the OR nurses, whose own clothing suddenly ignited.

The woman's agonized screams filled the room as her hair ignited like the tip of a lit match. As Frank Connor came pounding into the room he ran straight into the nurse. He shoved her to the floor and grabbed for a surgical blanket to beat out the flames.

McCabe took stock of the room. Cassidy's shirt was on fire, but he didn't seem to have noticed. He was trying to pat the flames out on Kellen with his bare hands. Hawkins and the rest of the medical staff were pulling the excruciatingly burned and dying Trimble to one side of the room.

McCabe ejected off the gurney, spraying flame on the curtains that hung along one wall as he moved. Instantly, noxious smoke filled the room and fire alarms started ringing. McCabe spat out the broken, bloody Narcan vial, a strip of dental floss still attached.

"It's Narcan, Doc," McCabe screamed, his eyes wild. "That stuff really works!" Then he was gone, racing through the clouds of smoke out into the corridor of the hospital and around a corner.

"Get him!" Cassidy screamed at Connor. "Go!"

McCabe was staring down a laundry chute set in the wall, the smooth stainless steel walls descending into the darkness of the hospital basement. His eyes swept the room, then he yanked open a cabinet and pulled out two rubber pads from a fibrillator machine. Without hesitation he jumped into the laundry chute, jamming the pads against the slick sides. He dropped fast and the paddles screeched from friction, but they slowed his fall enough. In a matter of seconds he vanished into the darkness in the depths of the building.

McCabe was gone by the time Frank got to the chute. Cassidy, however, was right behind him. He was ignoring his burns and had a furious look in his eye. His shirt hung on him in tatters.

"He go down there?" Cassidy yelled.

"I don't know—"

Cassidy pulled out his gun and fired three shots down the laundry chute, the slugs echoing and screaming off the steel sides.

"Stop," said Frank. "He's gone."

"Where did he go?" Marquez called as he came running into the room.

"No exits, Marquez?" Cassidy demanded.

‘‘That is not an exit,’’ Marquez replied, pointing at the open chute.

‘‘Well, McCabe sure as hell left through it,’’ said Cassidy. ‘‘Where does it lead?’’

‘‘The fall will kill him.’’

Cassidy grabbed Marquez by the shirtfront. ‘‘*Where does it lead, goddamnit!*’’

‘‘The laundry—in the basement,’’ said Marquez, pulling himself free. ‘‘It’s three floors down.’’

Cassidy grabbed the radio off his hip and keyed it. ‘‘Ten Henry fifty-five. Officer needs assistance. I want units to the basement now! Set a perimeter and lock down the hospital!’’ He turned and raced back toward the operating room.

Samantha Hawkins was struggling to restore some kind of order. She pounced on Cassidy.

‘‘We need help getting these people to ER,’’ she said. Trimble was a bloody mess, his chest, face, and hair burned. The nurse was in shock.

‘‘Not my job,’’ said Cassidy, pushing past her. But Samantha Hawkins was in no mood to be pushed around. She grabbed Cassidy by the tail of his tattered suit coat and yanked him back.

‘‘These are your men!’’ she said indignantly. ‘‘One of them is about to die!’’

For a moment, Cassidy looked angry enough to hit her, then he got hold of himself and grudgingly started to help move the injured onto gurneys. But then some uniformed cops came rushing in and Cassidy bolted, taking a couple of the policemen with him.

‘‘You, you, and you,’’ he yelled, ‘‘each take an elevator. The rest divide the two staircases.’’ He grabbed his radio again. "Tell Webster to locate the suspect on the tracking device." Cassidy clipped the radio back on his belt and looked around. "Where's Connor?"

But Frank Connor was long gone, already off and running, pounding down the fire stairs.

chapter 10

From a mountain of bags stuffed with sheets and soiled laundry, McCabe emerged like a sea monster. Then he took a step and almost fell—he had forgotten that his ankles were still shackled.

"Dammit," he hissed as he rifled the bales of laundry. He found a relatively clean lab coat and put it on over his orange prison jumpsuit. He crept to the door of the laundry room and peaked out. He had two things on his mind—the shackles and the locator device lodged in his own body. Noiselessly he stole out into the dimly lit corridor.

Frank raced down the corridor, a low-ceilinged passage lit only by periodic bare bulbs and flanked by pipes and electrical conduits. Ahead of him were the double swinging doors of the hospital laundry.

He went through them cautiously, gun drawn, the barrel sweeping the dimly lit room. Quickly he checked the room, kicking through the pile of soiled laundry, inspecting every nook and cranny. No McCabe.

At that moment Peter McCabe was only yards away, in a basement supply room foraging for anything that might be useful. He found a tray of scalpels next to a sterilization machine. He grabbed and pocketed a scalpel before he stepped into the adjoining room, acting as casual as he could.

This was the employees' locker room and it seemed to be empty. McCabe whistled "Moon River" as he went through the lockers looking for more useful items, but the only thing he could pick up was an apple, which he ate quickly. While he was chomping away at it, a young man came rushing into the room, threw open his locker, and started putting on his street clothes over his scrubs.

McCabe smiled and ambled over to him. "Crazy night, huh? What is going on up there? Any idea?"

"Hell if I know." The man's name was stamped over the pocket of his scrubs. Arthur Jones.

"Cops all over the place?"

"Everywhere, man. Everywhere. I just want to get the hell out of here before they go and volunteer my ass, you know?"

"I hear you, Arthur," said McCabe. "I want out of here myself." He fingered the scalpel in his pocket.

Frank Connor raced down the corridor and burst through a set of doors, running straight into Cassidy, Marquez, and a couple of other cops. There was instant chaos. The cops, startled and jumpy, sprang into shooting positions, pointing their weapons at Frank and screaming orders.

"Freeze!"

"Get your hands up!"

Frank raised up his hands. "I'm on the job! I'm a cop! I'm a cop!"

Time seemed to stand still for a long, long moment. And Frank realized he was one itchy finger away from being blown away. Then everyone relaxed and the men lowered their weapons.

"You find him?" Cassidy demanded.

"No. He's gone. He's not down there." He jerked a thumb toward the doors of the laundry room. "I checked it out."

"Where'd he go? How did he get out?" asked Cassidy angrily.

"There are no exits down here except for this," said Marquez.

"Unless he went back up the chute," said Frank. "And he didn't."

"Jesus Christ!" Cassidy grabbed the radio again. "Where do you have him now on the tracker?"

"The suspect is out of the perimeter," came the reply. The surprise in the techie's voice was evident. "I repeat—he is out of the perimeter."

Cassidy stared at the walkie-talkie, as if he wanted to kill it with his eyes. "Out?" he screamed. "Out? What do you mean *out?*"

"He is one thousand meters northwest of the building and moving away from the hospital—"

"Get the chopper ready," Cassidy barked into the radio. "Get it ready now!"

The whole pack of cops started heading for the stairs, Frank Connor following.

"Jerry, keep him alive, please," Connor pleaded. "Alive, please."

Cassidy turned and looked at him coldly. "You're not part of this, Frank," he said angrily. "Go take care of your kid."

Cassidy was wrong, of course. Frank was more a part of this whole thing than anyone else involved. He raced up the stairs and out the front door of the hospital. The air was loud with the sound of the chopper powering up on the hospital roof, but Frank paid no attention to it. He ran to the line of police cruisers parked at the curb and flashed his badge at one of the uniformed cops sitting behind the wheel of one of the cars.

"Move over!" Frank yelled at the cop, waving his ID card in his face.

"Hey! No one said anything about—"

"The prisoner is out!" Frank shouted. "Now move it!"

The young cop scooted over in the seat, a look of complete bafflement on his face. Frank jumped behind the wheel, twisted the key, then hit the gas and gunned the car away, scattering the news crews who were hanging around the entrance of the hospital.

Both Dawn Yoshioka and Sarah Davis watched the police car race away, then turned to each other.

"What was that all about?" Dawn wondered aloud. "Any ideas?"

Sarah stuck to the script as she had written it.

"We do not have any announcement from Captain Cassidy, but as soon as we do . . ."

But no one was paying any attention to her. The entire press corps was staring up at the roof of the hospital. Six stories above the street the helicopter was lifting off with a loud clatter.

Dawn turned back to Sarah. "You know, I don't think things are going to plan. . . ."

chapter 11

The chopper was in the air and police cars were fanning out below, racing to the directions being relayed by the techie running the tracker. He was with Cassidy in the helicopter, hunched over the control panel.

"Forty west by seventeen south," the techie announced through the mike in his headset. The direction was picked up by the central dispatch desk of the police department and then relayed to all cars.

"All units, suspect is heading south on 280," came out of the radio in the cruiser that Frank Connor was driving.

Frank was approaching the 280 South entrance to the freeway. He gritted his teeth and yanked the wheel and cut across three lanes of traffic, burning rubber up the ramp. He hit a hundred miles an hour the instant he was on the freeway, threading through traffic like a madman. He was glancing in the windows of the cars he passed. He looked up at a bus, but couldn't see much.

The chopper swooped and spun, the techie watching the scanner as best he could. "Thirty-two west by forty-one south. . . ." He looked out the window of the chopper, scanning the highway beneath him. "It's got to be one of those three vehicles down there. The bus or the two cars flanking it."

Frank had pushed the cruiser up to a hundred and ten. The young cop next to him was sure that he was about to die. He struggled to get his seat belt on.

"What did he say?" Frank yelled.

"He said it was one of those cars or the bus."

Frank looked in the rearview mirror—the bus and the two cars next to it were hundreds of yards behind him and getting smaller. He had passed them as if they had been standing still. The bus had a turn signal on and it was making for an exit Frank had long since passed.

The techie's voice came in clear. "It's the bus."

"Shit!" said Frank. Then he did what he had to do. He hit the siren and the light bar and then yanked the screaming car hard right. The cruiser hurtled across four lanes of traffic then smashed through the guardrail. The car was bucking like a bronco as it surged down the steep hill.

At the base of the hill the police cruiser careened straight across the frontage road, the front end of the machine slamming the pavement in a bright, wild explosion of sparks.

Traffic was bearing down on them as Frank gunned the engine, pushing every ounce of power from the cruelly abused engine. The front end of the car slammed into a parked car and came to a lurching halt. The uniformed cop came within inches of slamming his head into the windshield.

Frank pumped the ignition and jammed down on the accelerator, trying to restart the engine. "You okay?"

The young policeman was so shaken he could barely get the words out. "What in God's name is going on?"

"They implanted a tracking transmitter," said Connor quickly. "It's in McCabe's thigh or something."

Up ahead, the bus was slowing for a stop. Suddenly Frank bolted from the car and began sprinting toward it. He could see that the bus was crowded with San Franciscans heading home after a day's work. The passengers were reading newspapers or staring into space, completely unaware of the drama that was unfolding around them.

Frank could see that two passengers were getting off, that one was waiting to get on. As he reached the very rear of the bus the single man was climbing the steps. Then the front and rear doors closed with a pneumatic wheeze. With a puff of exhaust the heavy vehicle continued on its route.

Frank lunged, getting his fingers hooked inside the rear doors, his right foot on the step. But the bus was picking up speed and carrying him along. Frank yanked with all the strength he had, pulling the rear door open. An alarm screamed and the driver slammed on the brakes, throwing the passengers forward in their seats.

Frank pulled himself into the bus as if hauling himself out of the sea and into a boat.

The driver was coming down the aisle. He did not look happy. "Hell, mister, there's a bus every ten minutes. You could have just—" He stopped speaking when he saw the gun in Frank's hand.

Slowly Frank made his way forward, checking every passenger. There was an old lady, a couple of kids, some commuter types . . . and a man sitting slumped down in his seat, his collar turned up.

"You!" Frank raised his gun. A woman screamed when she saw the firearm. Arthur Jones, the hospital orderly—the guy with the upturned collar—blanched and winced. He raised his hands slowly. Frank saw that he was wearing hospital scrubs under his coat.

"Stay cool, man, okay?" Arthur managed to say. "Nobody wants any shooting, okay?"

In an instant, Frank knew what was going on. He plunged a hand into one of the coat pockets and pulled out a joint, a book of matches, and the transmitter still sticky with McCabe's blood. Frank felt sick—McCabe was so desperate that he had cut the transmitter out of his own body.

Arthur thought this was all about a joint. "Oh, come on, man, it's just a number somebody laid on me without my—"

But Frank Connor was already running off the bus, pounding back to the police cruiser.

The young cop was writing up the damaged car when Frank got back, and he had no time to get in before Connor started the cruiser up and drove away.

As he raced down the road he grabbed the mike on the radio and keyed it.

"It's not McCabe," he said.

In the chopper there were some confused looks from Cassidy and the rest. "Who the hell is that?"

"He wasn't on the bus," Frank announced. "He cut the transmitter out and dumped it."

From the chopper they could see the police cruiser zooming back toward the hospital. "Get Marquez. Have him seal every exit at the hospital. Tell him it's Cassidy's order."

Cassidy, up there in the helicopter, felt as if his crazy world had just become a degree crazier. "*My* orders?" He grabbed the microphone. "Who is that? Is that you, Connor? Frank? Is that you?"

Frank was back on the highway and doing a hundred back toward the hospital. He paid no attention to Cassidy's voice.

"I told you to stay out of this!" Cassidy screamed. "You're too—" Frank did not take his eyes off the road as he reached over and switched off the radio, interrupting Cassidy's tirade in mid-sentence.

chapter 12

McCabe had gotten rid of one problem—the transmitter—now he was taking care of another. For the ten or fifteen minutes that the San Francisco Police Department thought he was out of the building, Peter McCabe had been lucky enough to have free run of the upper floors of the hospital. In Dermatology and Special Surgeries he found what he was looking for—a laser machine and a young man who knew how to operate it. The young man was unwilling to help until McCabe had shown him the error of his ways by quickly and painfully beating some sense into him, reducing, with a few hard blows, the laser technician's face to a bloody pulp.

Even so, McCabe kept the technician in a tight headlock as he laid his legs on the treatment table.

There was a wide patch of blood on McCabe's leg where he had cut out the locator transmitter.

"You're not going to get far on that leg," the laser technician said. His concern was touching considering he spoke through split and bloody lips, provided courtesy of Peter McCabe.

"Your concern is noted and appreciated," said McCabe. The blade of the laser—the concentrated band of light—was usually used for more delicate tasks like dermabrasion or doing precise plastic surgery work, but it took on the hardened tungsten of McCabe's shackles without problem, slicing through the metal as easily as doing an eye job on a Pacific Heights dowager.

In fewer than five minutes he was free of the shackles and on his way. The laser technician was permitted to live—he was in no condition to be a threat to McCabe.

He had no trouble blending in with the army of workers in the hospital. The only thing that set McCabe off from the other orderlies and nurses was the bloodstain on his thigh and his slight limp—but no one looked twice at a bloodstain in a hospital.

Spotting an ambulance driver walking down the hall, an EMS hat on his head, McCabe decided it was time for another change of disguise. . . .

Frank Connor had made it back to the hospital in record time. Security was tight and getting tighter as the perimeter was reestablished, and Frank figured his best shot at getting back into the building was through the emergency room, but he was stopped before he could get to the wide double doors.

"Hey, where do you think you're going?" said a uniformed cop who pounced on him as he ran for the entrance to the ER.

Frank had his badge out. "I've got to get in there. *Now.*"

"Sorry, man," said the cop's partner. "You can't go in. Orders from Captain Cassidy himself."

"I'm Connor," said Frank desperately. "My son is inside there."

There was some kind of commotion behind them, a man shouting: "Hey! That guy! He stole my hat!"

Frank looked from the cops to the emergency room doors and saw McCabe ambling out through them, the EMS hat pulled down low on his brow. He was fifteen feet from freedom when he saw Frank.

"That's him!" Connor yelled and broke for the doors as McCabe turned around and walked straight back into the hospital.

As the doors swept open, Frank Connor ran smack into the ambulance driver—McCabe had hooked the man under the arms and flung him at the cop—and both of them tumbled to the floor. Frank was on his feet in an instant.

"It's McCabe!" he yelled. "He's *there.* Get him!"

But the two cops on the door had their orders, and held Frank back by the shoulders. "It's orders, man.

You can't go in there!"

"Let me go, please," Frank pleaded. "We're losing him!"

The commotion at the front door had attracted the attention of Marquez, who saw the struggle on the monitor up in the command post.

An instant later Marquez himself appeared. "Let him go!" He reached down and yanked Frank to his feet. "Where is he?"

"McCabe . . ." said Frank breathlessly, "he just went up in the elevator."

"Jesus!" said Marquez angrily. "Come on!" He ran down the hall, leading the way back to the command post.

Both men hunched over the bank of monitors as various images flashed on the screens, showing different parts of the hospital. Nothing seemed amiss.

"We've got sixteen stories, a million square feet, over a thousand rooms, eleven different elevator banks and stairwells," said Marquez grimly. "We're not going to find him by running around the place looking under the beds and in closets."

"Jesus!" said Frank Connor. "As long as he stays in the building . . ."

"They've got the outside secured," Marquez replied. "He's not going anywhere. But we've got to evacuate as many people as possible so they can conduct a search."

Frank nodded. "Yeah, yeah . . . I know. It's just that—"

Marquez nodded and smiled understandingly. "Hey, if it was my kid, I'd be going a little crazy too."

A drop of blood—just a drop—had formed inside Matt's nose, but that tiny red bead suggested a whole raft of medical problems. The boy was sleeping and his breathing remained steady and calm under the clear plastic of the oxygen tent that now covered his bed. But the lack of coagulation in his blood was a troubling development. Even Nate, still on guard, could tell that it was not a good sign.

Outside, in the corridor, Nate could hear the sound of footsteps and he reached for his gun, tensing as he watched the handle of the door twist.

Then Frank slipped into the room and Nate relaxed, shaking his head and exhaling heavily. "Man, will I be glad when this is all over."

"That makes two of us." Frank stared down at his son. "How's he doing?"

"Sleeping," said Nate. "What's going on out there? I've heard sirens, choppers. . . ."

"McCabe is still in the hospital," Frank replied. "Be careful."

"Dad?" Matt's voice was weak and muffled by the plastic of the oxygen tent. Frank was at the bedside in an instant. He wanted to reach inside and hold his son's hand, but he knew he could not. He put his hand up to the plastic and Matt touched the other side, as if measuring his own small hand against his father's.

"Something went really wrong, didn't it?" Matt asked softly.

Frank nodded. "Yeah . . . I'm afraid it did. Sorry. . . ."

There were dark points of disappointment in Matt's eyes. "So I guess I'm not going to get my operation then, am I?"

Frank saw the droplet of blood in Matt's nose, but he did his best to conceal his alarm. "Yes, you are," he said, hoping he sounded reassuring. "You'll get the operation, Matt. I promise."

Matt smiled and nodded, but Frank could not tell if his son believed him. "Go to sleep," said Frank. "And I'll be back when I can."

Matt did as he was told, closing his eyes and settling down further in the bed. Frank turned to Nate, his voice low so his son would not hear.

"I've got to go find Hawkins," he said, heading for the door. "He needs help."

"I know," said Nate soberly. He sat down next to the bed again and realized that Matt was staring up at him, not even trying to go to sleep.

Nate smiled. "So, who do you like better, Deana Troy or Tasha Yar?"

Matt did his best to laugh. They had been playing this game for as long as Matt could remember. Both he and Nate had a voluminous knowledge of *Star Trek* and they were always trying to one-up each other.

"Come on, Nate, Tasha's been dead for years. Executed by Romulans. And Deana Troy—she's a Betazoid." He thought for a moment then he added shyly: "I think Jadzia Dax is kind of pretty, though.'' It was not an easy admission for a nine-year-old to make, girls having only recently left the ''icky'' zone.

Nate looked surprised. ''A Trill? Puh-leeze. Get serious.''

chapter 13

The only part of the hospital still open and functioning was the emergency room, but things there were like a barely controlled riot. Doctors and nurses were working at a fever pitch as they tried to deal with the havoc caused by McCabe's escape.

Behind a curtain, though, in a far corner of the room, the author of all this murder and disaster was hiding. He was calmly performing surgery on himself. Ignoring the pain, he worked at suturing himself, closing the wound where he had torn out the transmitter. He was surprisingly adept, slipping the needle in and out of his own skin, his hands rock steady. He did not even wince as he broke off the surgical thread, then blotted the blood with a towel.

Beyond the curtain the noise of the emergency room pulsed, with Samantha Hawkins's voice carrying above the mayhem.

"We need another ten of morphine!" she ordered. "And get him to pre-op. Now!"

McCabe dared to peek out from his hiding place and saw Hawkins bent over a steel gurney, examining the wounds of one of the burned policemen. The cop's face and arms had been burned raw.

A young nurse, the strain of her worst day ever on the job plain on her face, hurried to do Dr. Hawkins's bidding, running toward the supply room for the extra vials of morphine.

"The burn unit is swamped," Hawkins told the cop. "I'll take care of you here myself."

It was all the cop could do to nod, the pain too great to allow him to speak. Hawkins knew that he had to be sedated or the shock of the pain was going to start shutting down his vital organs.

Hawkins looked up sharply. "Nurse! I am still waiting for—"

The nurse was frozen in the middle of the room, a few steps from the door of the supply room, a morphine drip in her hand.

"What's the matter with you?" Hawkins snapped. "We've got an emergency here and you're—"

The curtain from the treatment cubicle behind Hawkins billowed open and McCabe's arm yanked her back. His other hand rested the blade of the scalpel lightly against her throat. McCabe smiled at the nurse. The woman still had not moved.

"She's right about the emergency," said McCabe. "But you shouldn't let Dr. Hawkins yell at you like that. It's bad for self-esteem. You'll lose your self-respect, you know?"

The nurse still had not moved a muscle and was

staring at McCabe as if she had been hypnotized by a swaying snake. She did not even flinch when Frank Connor strode into the room. At first all he saw was Dr. Hawkins and the nurse.

"Dr. Hawkins, I think Matt's platelets are low," he said. "He's bleeding from the— Jesus!" He saw McCabe and whipped out his gun, crouching low, looking for some shred of cover.

McCabe did not seem too upset to see Frank Connor. "Dr. Hawkins . . . tell the father of your patient what will happen when you try to take bone marrow from a dead person."

Hawkins was silent, even as McCabe jabbed the edge of the scalpel into the skin on her neck. "Tell him, Doctor. Now."

Hawkins spoke, but she didn't say what she had been instructed to say. Instead she addressed everyone in the emergency room, the nurses and orderlies working on patients.

"Move all the patients into the hallway. Stop what you are doing and move them. *At once*."

"Bitch!" McCabe's anger got the better of him this time and he yanked her back by a handful of hair and he smacked her forehead against the edge of the gurney frame.

"McCabe!" Connor shouted. "Let her go!"

McCabe, of course, did no such thing. Instead he bared her neck and pressed the scalpel hard against her carotid artery. "I am not afraid to die, Frank. So you know I am not afraid to kill her. You understand that, don't you?"

Hawkins did not seem to have been infected by the fear or the tension that had suffused the room.

"The moment he dies, his marrow dies," she said evenly. "It coagulates and becomes useless to Matt."

Something in her calm manner suggested that the pain in her head was irrelevant—despite the bruise rapidly forming on her forehead—and the directness of her gaze established an almost palpable link between her and Frank.

"How do you think you're going to get out of here, McCabe?" Frank said. He knew there was practically no chance of talking McCabe out of the situation, but he wanted at least to give it a shot.

"That's my problem, not yours. Now, I'm counting to five in my head, and your gun will be on the floor or your son's doctor will be dead. . . . I've started counting, Frank."

Connor had already spotted a gun and holster lying on the floor of a cubicle—the weapon of one of the burned cops. Slightly reassured, Frank slowly placed his gun on the floor.

"I'm putting it down," Frank said, keeping his voice calm. "Now talk to me, McCabe. Let's make a deal now. Okay?"

McCabe smirked. "A deal? Great. What can you offer me, Frank? Eternal life? Without the possibility of parole?" He shook his head slowly. "No deals, Frank." McCabe turned to the nurse. "Pull that curtain for me, will you, honey."

The nurse leaped to do as McCabe had told her and as the curtain billowed out McCabe saw the holstered gun Frank had earlier spotted. McCabe smiled and almost wagged a finger at Frank.

"You can pass that gun holster over here too,

honey. . . . Oh, and Frank, kick your gun over here. And don't do anything heroic. I'm counting down in my head again."

"I can't do that," said Frank. "My gun stays right here. . . . Listen, maybe I can get you privileges at the prison."

"Cigarettes for freedom, Frank? What kind of deal is that?" He shook his head slowly. "Now send that gun over here."

To Frank's—and everyone's—surprise the petrified nurse kicked Frank's gun across the floor, where it stopped a few feet in front of McCabe. She also knelt and slid over the weapon of the injured cop.

In Frank's line of sight he could see two cops, Wilson and Raines, inching into the emergency room. He could tell what the cops were going to do. They would pounce, fire, and let the chips fall where they may. They would get McCabe and Hawkins too, probably. But they would also be taking Matt.

"Stop!" Frank ordered loudly. "He's got Doctor Hawkins."

The cops stopped short as McCabe yanked back the curtain and grinned at Wilson and Raines. He pressed the scalpel to Hawkins's throat.

"Okay, cowboys, drop the guns. And you"—McCabe cocked a chin at Raines—"take off that headset and toss it here."

Raines slid over the headset, but he kept the gun. Both cops kept their guns rock steady, aimed at him, ready to take him down.

"Wilson! You kill him, you kill my son!" Frank yelled. "Please!"

Wilson did not even look at Frank. Instead he

muttered into the headset mike, "He's in the ER. The emergency room. We have him!"

"Don't be a hero," Frank said, his teeth clenched. "He's got no place to go."

McCabe nodded. "That's right. Listen to the man. I got no place to go. So put your guns down, 'cause if you even twitch, I'm gonna have to kill the good doctor here." McCabe was silent for a moment. "But Wilson, he's thinking: I shoot him right in the kneecap, he doubles over crippled. I save the girl . . . but the convict is still alive. Everybody's happy. Something like that, right, Wilson?"

The cop glowered at him. McCabe smiled back. "But I want you to note how we are standing, her head against my shoulder, the scalpel just so. . . . I get shot, physics and gravity are gonna make me slice right through her carotid artery. How fast will you die, Doctor? How fast?"

"Two minutes," said Hawkins matter-of-factly. "A little less, perhaps."

"Twoooo minutes," said McCabe tauntingly. "That's not a long time."

"I'm warning you, McCabe," Wilson growled. "Let her go and—"

"You're warning *me?*" McCabe retorted. "I'm warning *you*, you dumb fuck. You kill me, I kill her and little Frank Junior dies with us. How's that going to look in the papers? You won't be a hero, you'll be one more trigger-happy argument for a Civilian Review Board."

McCabe's ridicule infuriated Wilson and Frank could see the muscles in the cop's neck bulge in fury. Frank could sense that the tension in the room was going to break—and break disastrously. Without thinking about it, Frank moved into Wilson's line of fire, protecting both McCabe and Hawkins. But Frank couldn't block Raines at the same time.

McCabe watched calmly, and under the cover of the momentary drama he reached for Frank's gun still on the floor near his feet.

Frank's eyes were on Wilson now. "Just go, McCabe—he won't shoot."

"But if I let the doc go, they'll kill me—and then what will happen to Matt?" He was looking at Frank and Wilson thought he had the opening he had been waiting for.

"Raines! Now!" Wilson shouted.

McCabe shoved Hawkins into Frank, diving for Frank's gun as Raines squeezed off a shot and missed, the bullet slamming into the wall. In one fluid motion, McCabe got hold of Connor's gun, raised it, and fired once. The bullet caught Raines dead square in the middle of the forehead and dropped him in an instant.

Wilson's nerve had broken. He fired, but he fired wide and panicky, emptying his gun in McCabe's general direction. McCabe—not panicked—aimed, fired, and hit Wilson in the chest. The cop flew backward, slamming into the wall.

Frank came up with a gun in his hand. McCabe stopped and smirked. He was standing framed in the door, a perfect target.

"Go ahead, Frank. Shoot me."

But Frank could not do it. McCabe knew he couldn't do it. He could not resist another long chuckle. Then he shouted to Wilson. The cop was alive and conscious, but hurt bad. He was sure that he could hear him, though.

"See, Wilson, if you'd let me go, your buddy would be alive, you'd be healthy, and I'd be out of here just like I am anyway. . . ."

Then he was gone.

chapter 14

Raines was dead. Hawkins's practiced eye told her that in an instant so she concentrated on Wilson, mopping at the ugly wound in his chest with a towel. The cloth under her hands was turning red and warm. Frank stood between the two men, torn between going after McCabe and the sight of two fellow cops—one dead, the other, perhaps dying. Wilson looked up at him. He had difficulty breathing, but there was no mistaking the look of hatred in his eyes.

"You gave up your gun," he said.

They both knew it was the cardinal sin for any cop. But before Frank could say a word in his own defense, Cassidy raced into the room with a group of cops.

"We had him," Wilson gasped. As he lost blood he was losing consciousness. "We had McCabe.

Connor let him go." Wilson winced in pain. "Ah Jesus!"

Cassidy and the other cops looked at Frank Connor as if he had just committed treason. Frank raised his hands weakly, not even bothering to try to explain.

"Get McCabe," Cassidy ordered his men. "Go *get him now!"*

"Gas him, tranquilize him," Frank Connor pleaded, "but don't—"

Cassidy yanked the gun out of Frank's hand. "I told you to stay out of it," he said. He was so consumed with fury that his voice was barely audible. "Now you're finished."

"What the hell would you have done?" Frank asked angrily.

"I got a son too," snarled Cassidy. "So did that man's mother." He pointed at Raines. "Everybody who dies here, you killed them. You. Because you let your personal feelings affect your judgment." He grabbed two uniformed cops and waved them over. "I want Connor locked up till this is over."

"Awww, Jerry," said Frank. "C'mon. There's no need for that."

The two uniforms got on either side of him and took him by the arm. They started pulling him away.

"No cuffs, until you get by the press," said Cassidy, as if he was offering Frank a deal. "Now get the hell out of here."

"I'll go to Matt," said Hawkins. "He'll be okay with me. Don't worry."

Frank nodded. "Tell him— Tell him I'll . . ." But he couldn't think of anything to tell him. Hawkins nodded, understanding his confusion and her inability to act to help him. As the two cops pulled him away, though, Hawkins thought that Frank looked calm, collected, almost as if he was planning something.

Cassidy was back in full cop mode. "Complete the evacuation in the search zones," he shouted into his radio handset. "And bring in the dogs."

Frank Connor went quietly, the two cops leading him through the emergency room and out to the front of the hospital.

A lot was going on out there. Police crime scene tape was everywhere, sealing off the forecourt of the building. Searchlights were being set up and an ever growing ring of San Francisco Police Department officers were busy keeping the ever growing press pool at bay.

As Frank emerged, he could see that an orderly evacuation of noncritical-care patients was underway. Men and women were being wheeled to ambulances, loaded in, and then sent to medical sites all over the Bay Area. A police car drew up and the two cops hustled Frank toward it.

Then, in the knot of press, he spotted Dawn Yoshioka. "Dawn! Dawn! Over here!" The woman looked around wildly, trying to locate the source of the voice. Then she saw him and she and her crew started to run toward him.

"Dawn!" Frank yelled. "Don't believe the police. They're lying to you. I'll tell you what's really going on inside!"

Like sharks to blood, the stampede of reporters

began, Dawn leading the pack. Suddenly the two cops and Frank were engulfed in a pushing, kicking mass of TV reporters, microphones, and the lenses of video cameras. There was a cacophony of questions being shouted.

"Is McCabe alive? What were those gunshots? What about your son, Frank? Has the transplant taken place yet?"

The crowd was going wild. They had been waiting for hours and they knew something was up, but not a word had been leaked to them. The frustration boiled over and suddenly the reporters were shoving, bullying, thrusting, and crushing. It was more like a rugby scrum than an impromptu news conference. It was all the two cops could do to protect themselves, much less keep a firm grip on Frank. When one cop turned to fight off a cameraman, Frank struck, elbowing the uniform in the guts then bolting away as the man doubled over.

Frank broke free and sprinted to a neatly parked line of police motorcycles. He jumped on one of the giant machines and revved it and, before the other cops could even react, he took off down the street.

The other cop had a chance at grabbing him, but he got tangled up with a cameraman who was intent on filming the escape. In an instant the opportunity was gone and the cop shoved the cameraman aside.

"Goddamnit!" He grabbed his radio and shouted into it: "Son of a bitch! Connor's gone!"

Frank blasted around the corner on the motorcycle, then jammed it hard, accelerating straight up one of San Francisco's steep hills. At the top he took a hard right, then a left, then he hit the gas hard again and roared to the summit of the hill, a street thick with row houses divided by gardens.

He dismounted at the curb, turned off the big machine, then walked it a few feet up onto the sidewalk as if he were taking it up the walkway to the garage of one of the row houses. Halfway there, though, he let the big bike topple over, dumping it in the bushes where it could not be seen from the street.

Frank walked away quickly—not too quickly, not fast enough to arouse suspicion—but with a purpose in his step as if he were in a hurry to get someplace specific. And that was the truth—he had to find a way back into San Francisco Memorial Hospital.

The night seemed to be alive with sirens, the loud wails penetrating even into this peaceful residential neighborhood. The sirens were getting louder too and suddenly he saw a phalanx of police cars zooming up the hill coming toward him. He had no doubt who they were looking for.

The only cover was the open door of a Korean grocery store and he ducked in quickly, watching from inside as the police cars roared by. Once they were gone, Frank turned and saw that the owner was watching him suspiciously from behind the counter.

Frank smiled and began to browse in the merchandise. It was one of those corner grocery stores that sold everything—from food and drink, of course, to cleaning supplies, to pots and pans.

Suddenly, Frank had an idea.

chapter 15

The K-9 units of the San Francisco Police Department were cut loose and took off at a dead run, the scent from McCabe's bloody towel fixed in their brains. Cops followed closely, guns out.

The dogs were snarling now, sprinting down the corridor, scrabbling through a left turn, their claws snatching at the smooth linoleum. They were barking loudly as they charged past the operating rooms and toward the surgical supply rooms at the end of the hall.

The K-9 commander was yelling into his walkie-talkie. "We definitely have the scent! Repeat, the dogs have the scent!"

The dogs were baying and scratching at the supply room door and the cop kicked it in, the dogs streaming into the tiny chamber, howling and going crazy. They leaped up the wall, but not at McCabe.

The K-9 commander caught a quick glimpse of

the prey before the first dog's teeth sunk into it. It was a latex surgical glove, fat like a balloon and smeared with a gout of McCabe's blood.

The dogs sprung at it, viciously tearing it open. Suddenly the bag exploded, spurting liquid and filling the room with the noxious stink of ammonia. The caustic liquid spilled into the muzzles and eyes of the dogs and they screamed in pain.

"Ammonia!" shouted the K-9 cop. "That bastard!"

Frank had purchased the most peculiar collection of items in the Korean grocery. He started with a cheap aluminum cooking pan, then added a bottle of ketchup, a can of cranberry juice, and a bottle of cornstarch, all topped off with a dish towel.

He found an alley around the corner from the hospital and quickly mixed the ingredients together until they took on a blood-red color and a viscous, but slightly runny consistency. He poured the mixture on the dishcloth, then clapped the whole mess against his face and started walking toward the hospital.

As soon as he saw the first cops on the perimeter he let out a couple of deep, heartfelt groans.

"Oh Jesus," said one of the cops as Frank approached. "Catch this one."

"Hey, buddy," said the other one. "The hospital is closed. This place is not—"

Frank collapsed into the cop's arms, his face swathed in the bloody towel.

"Aww, shit," said the first cop.

"We better take him into the emergency room,"

said his partner. "If he dies on us—outside a hospital—we'll have lawsuits forever."

"Yeah, okay."

The two men hooked Frank under the shoulders and dragged him through the sliding doors of the emergency room. They were happy to hand him over to the first ER orderly they found.

"You want to take this guy?" said one of the cops.

"We're kinda busy, officers."

"Look," said the other cop, "he's probably dying. Let him croak in here, okay?"

They dumped Frank on a gurney, then, figuring their duty done, they walked out of the ER. The orderly sighed heavily, grabbed his clipboard, and ran through the usual set of questions:

"Were you shot? Were you stabbed? Were you beaten? Did you have a traffic accident? Did you fall and hurt yourself? Have you consumed poison? Have you consumed prescription drugs and/or alcohol? . . ."

But the only response the orderly got was a series of very eloquent groans from Frank Connor.

"I'll go get a doctor," said the orderly.

The instant the young man was gone, Frank sat up and stripped the towel from his face, using part of it to wipe the fake blood. He tossed the sodden rag aside and darted down the corridor.

There was a knock on Matt's door, but Nate was ready, gun in hand. "Yeah? Who is it?"

"It's me. Hawkins."

Nate unlocked the door quickly. "I'm glad to see *you*. He's bleeding more."

The doctor nodded and went straight to the bed. The phone rang and Nate snatched it up.

"It's me," said Frank. He was calling from a pay phone somewhere deep in the bowels of the deserted hospital.

"Oh man," said Nate, vastly relieved to hear his partner's voice. "I heard they threw you out of this place."

"They did," said Frank. "I'm back in. How's Matt doing? Is he still bleeding?"

Nate looked over at Hawkins. Her concern for her patient was obvious and she looked worried about the bleeding and Matt's increasingly labored breathing. She shook her head slowly.

"He needs platelets right away to help him coagulate," she said.

Nate did his best to lie. "He's fine," he said into the phone. "It's stopped."

Behind him the door opened and McCabe stole into the room. Without warning he cracked Nate on the back of the head with the handle of his gun. Nate tumbled to the floor.

Frank heard the commotion. "Nate? *Nate?*" All he heard was Hawkins's voice saying, "What the hell are you—" then the connection was broken. Frank raced for the stairs.

Dr. Hawkins had not been intimidated by McCabe before; she was not going to start now. She folded her arms across her chest and looked him square in the eye.

"I need some help, Doctor," said McCabe.

"Too bad," Hawkins spat back. "My patient needs me here."

McCabe raised the gun. "I'm afraid I need you more." He grabbed her arm and turned her toward the door. Then, for the first time, he caught a glimpse of Matt. The kid was weak, but he was straining to look over the side of the bed.

"Nate. . . . Nate. . . . What did you do to Nate?" said Matt. He was close to tears.

"He'll be okay," said McCabe gently. "Just a bump on the head."

Matt looked up at him and stared. "You're McCabe, aren't you?"

McCabe smiled, as if flattered at having been recognized. "That's right. And you're Matt. . . . Listen, I apologize. I only need your doctor for a minute. I'll send her right back, okay, Matt?"

"No," said Matt.

McCabe flashed him another smile, then steered Hawkins out into the hall.

"Where's the cyclopropane?" McCabe demanded.

Hawkins dug in the pocket of her lab coat and pulled out her computerized card key. "Here. You can take my card. It'll get you in anywhere."

McCabe's affable demeanor vanished in an instant. He grabbed a handful of her hair and slammed her against the wall, leaning in so that his face was barely an inch from hers. It was a posture at once threatening and sexual. Samantha tried to twist away, but he held her firm, tightening the grip on her hair.

"Listen," he hissed into her ear. "I like you. I

like everything about you. But I am trying to be a gentleman here. So let me ask you again, and you give me any more of that 'uh, duh, take my card but don't worry about the lock code' bullshit, I'll forget my manners. . . . Now, let's find the cyclopropane."

"Okay," Samantha Hawkins whispered.

McCabe grinned again. "That's better. Let's go, Doctor."

Hawkins turned and led him down the hall. As they went, McCabe dug the pack of cigarettes out of her coat pocket and lit one. "Tell me, Doctor," he said. "Give me your opinion: Do you think smoking is going to take years off my life?"

Cassidy had given in and called in the SFPD SWAT team. They arrived in their armored vehicles and started assembling their gear in the parking lot. They came well prepared, right down to a heavy, armor-plated personnel carrier mounted with machine gun and searchlight.

The SWAT commander went straight to Cassidy. He was focused and ready for the coming struggle, but calm too.

"Do we have any idea where he is?" he asked Cassidy.

"We know he's above the second floor."

The SWAT commander nodded. "I need to talk to the building engineer. I want blueprints and schematics for the whole place. I want all the keys."

Cassidy turned to one of his cops. "Do it. Now."

"If you can't find the engineer," the SWAT commander continued, "get me a janitor. They always know more than anybody." He lowered his voice.

"If we get a clear shot we're going to take him."

Cassidy nodded. "You kill McCabe, Connor's boy dies with him." It was as if he wanted to spread the blame a little.

The SWAT commander nodded. It was plain that he was sympathetic, but it just wasn't his problem.

Cassidy grabbed Marquez. "Where's Connor?"

"He got away from the two uniforms," Marquez reported. "He's at large."

"Like hell. If he got away he came straight back here." He looked over his shoulder at one of the SWAT cops. He was assembling a long-barreled sniper's rifle. He would be the man to take McCabe down if the target presented itself.

Cassidy didn't want Connor around if it came to that. "Find Connor and get him out of the building."

As it was a common anesthetic, there was always a lot of cyclopropane on hand in a hospital. For Peter McCabe's purpose, however, it was the highly flammable property of the gas that interested him.

Hawkins opened the supply cabinet that held the tanks of the gas, each stainless steel cylinder about the size of a small fire extinguisher. The tanks were covered with stickers that read: "Extremely flammable—contents under pressure."

"Could you pick up one of those?" McCabe asked Hawkins, nodding at one of the tanks.

Hawkins picked one up, watching as McCabe grabbed two more cyclopropane tanks as well as a smaller tank marked "liquid nitrogen."

"Good," said McCabe politely. "Now would you please lead me to the main electrical room."

"If I have to."

"You have to," said McCabe firmly.

Hawkins turned as if to do as she was told, then, with all the power she could muster, she swung the tank, cracking the canister hard against McCabe's knee. He screamed in pain and dropped his tanks, the noise of the metal hitting the concrete floor drowned out by his bellow.

Unbalanced by the blow and the pain, he fell backward, but Hawkins wasn't finished with him. She had a pen in her hand and she jabbed it into the freshly sutured wound in his thigh, breaking the stitches. He screamed again and fell to the floor, the gun falling from his hand. Hawkins grabbed it and ran.

Matt had pulled himself out of the sterile tent and was half out of the bed, but did not have the strength to climb down completely.

"Nate? Nate?" Matt whispered. "Nate, wake up."

But Nate groaned on the floor and didn't quite make it back to consciousness. Matt breathed deeply and started gathering his strength to climb out of the bed to make it to the telephone.

Then Frank burst into the room. "Dad!" Matt cried, relief flooding through him.

"Don't touch anything!" Frank ordered. "And get back under that tent."

Matt obeyed instantly, as if he knew that the slightest contamination could infect him. Frank squatted over Nate and tapped his cheeks. "Nate, come on. . . ."

Nate groaned and his eyes fluttered open. "Jesus, man. . . ."

"What happened?" Frank asked.

"McCabe paid us a visit," said Nate groggily.

"He took Dr. Hawkins," Matt gasped from the bed.

Frank jumped to his feet and leaned over the bed. He saw the blood on his son's nose and the sudden realization of the danger Matt was in hit him like a truck. His face fell.

Matt couldn't help but notice the look on his father's face. "Dad, what's the matter?"

"Nothing," Frank said quickly. "Nothing. Where did he take her?"

Matt shook his head. "I don't know. . . . He asked her where the propane something was, you know, like propane for cooking?"

"Cyclopropane," said Frank. "Nate, you okay here?"

Nate got to his feet, nodding. But Frank was already gone.

In the hallway, Hawkins and Frank Connor almost collided.

"Where is he?"

She pointed back down the corridor the way she had come. "He was by the storage closet, down there to the right," she said, slightly out of breath. "He's got cyclopropane."

"I know that."

"I ripped out his stitches," she said and smiled.

"I didn't know that"—Frank turned back toward his son's room—"Matt's got the—"

Hawkins nodded vigorously. "I know. He needs Amicar and I'm going to have to get to the pharmacy for that." She handed over the gun, as if she had found something he had misplaced. "I think this is yours."

Frank was startled and impressed. So far Samantha Hawkins was the only person to have taken on Peter McCabe and triumphed.

"I have to get to the pharmacy." But as she started to go, Frank took her by the arm.

"Don't call the cops," he said soberly.

"Why not?"

"They'll kill McCabe on sight."

She knew it was true and he knew that he was asking a lot of her. It was big moment; they both realized that they were crossing the line now. Finally Samantha Hawkins nodded. "Okay," she said. "No police."

chapter 16

Hawkins retrieved the supply of the coagulant from the deserted pharmacy and was hurrying back along the corridor when she got caught in a sweep through the floor by SWAT cops.

"This section of the hospital is locked down," said the team leader, surprised to find anyone up there on that level. "No one is permitted up here. You coulda gotten shot, lady."

"That's *doctor,*" Hawkins snapped. "And I have a dying patient who needs this drug right now." She waved the box of Amicar under the guy's nose. "Am I permitted to attend him?" She tried to push past him, but he grabbed her arm, stopping her.

"I am just—"

"Just following orders, I know," said Hawkins. "Why don't you take me to whoever is giving them?"

There was nothing the cop would rather do than

pass this particular problem along to his immediate superior. "Doctor, that's exactly where we're going."

Cassidy was not pleased to see the SWAT team bring Hawkins into the command post. "Where the hell did she come from?"

"Found her up on five," said the SWAT team leader.

"Well, don't let her out of here," Cassidy said brusquely. He turned his back on her, but Hawkins grabbed him and spun him around.

"Do you understand what I'm telling you, you fucking moron?" she yelled. "The boy's life is in danger. He has got to be medicated immediately!"

Cassidy was just as angry as she was and in no mood to be intimidated. He looked at her coldly and spoke slowly. "Doctor, how many people are going to have to die tonight so that kid can live?"

Drops of blood led down the corridor away from the storage closet. McCabe was lugging the cyclopropane in a canvas sack, unaware that he was leaving a perfect trail in his wake.

He stopped in front of a gray metal door emblazoned with warnings: *Electrical—Keep Out* and *Danger—High Voltage*

As he lowered the sack to the floor he looked back to see if he was being followed and saw the trail of blood drops. McCabe knew it was bad, but there was nothing he could do about it now.

Working quickly he uncapped a canister of the liquid nitrogen and shot the liquid into and around the door lock. The metal parts froze instantly, the lock becoming brittle.

Then McCabe threw the full weight of his shoulder against the door; the frozen lock parts shattered like glass. Yanking open the door he surveyed the tangle of cables and junction boxes cemented to the walls.

Next came the cyclopropane. McCabe unscrewed the first tank and sloshed the unatomized liquid all over the electrical cables, the switches, the panels. Despite the fire hazard, he had a cigarette in his mouth and he was puffing on it, heedless of the chance of stray sparking, as if he didn't really care if he blew himself up.

But Frank Connor did. He was about forty feet down the hall, gun drawn, watching as McCabe rigged his makeshift bomb.

"Stop right there, McCabe."

McCabe's head popped out of the closet. "Frank!"

"On the ground, now," Frank ordered sternly. "Arms out."

McCabe took a big drag on his cigarette. "I'm getting bored, Frank. You couldn't shoot me last time. How's this gonna be any—"

Frank let fly with two shots, the bullets slamming through the door at about knee height. "Don't give me any bullshit about physics and gravity, McCabe. I can shoot to disable. Now get down on the floor."

"Okay, okay. . . ." He came out from behind the door, his hands up, the cigarette in one of them. Then, with a smile on his face he dropped the butt.

They both watched as the glowing tip of the cigarette fell into the trail of cyclopropane.

There was a flash, then a ball of fire blew down the hallway, filling the narrow space, wall to wall. There was a strange silence as the fire momentarily sucked all the oxygen from the room, but Frank knew enough to hit the floor, feeling the heat wash over him, singeing his hair and clothes. The fireball was gone in an instant. Then the lights flickered and went out. McCabe was gone.

The lights flickered in the command post too, then went dark as the short circuit blew through the entire system. No one was watching Samantha—she grabbed a radio and raced out into the darkened corridor.

"Nate? Nate, can you hear me?" she whispered into the handset of the walkie-talkie.

Matt's room was in darkness and the ventilation fan in the oxygen tent had stopped. Nate felt around in the darkness, searching for the radio. His hand closed around it.

"Doc! Where are you? The electricity is out, the ventilator, everything is out."

Matt was awake and really frightened now. "What's happening, Nate?"

"It'll be okay," said Nate, doing his best to sound reassuring.

"You've got to get him into someplace clean," said Hawkins urgently. She thought for a moment. "The infectious disease lab, there's an isolation ward there. I don't think there's anyone there."

Nate nodded to himself. "Yeah, in the old building. I've seen the plans." He shot a quick smile at Matt. "So how do we get there?"

"Via the walkway. There's a lock. The code is 7595. I'll get the amino caproic and meet you there."

"Okay," said Nate. He looked at the bed. It was on thick rubber wheels. "Well, Matt, looks like we're going for a ride."

Warden Fayne entered the police command post just as the backup and emergency lights kicked in. Marquez set his monitor to inspect a section of the grid.

"We got redundant emergency systems," Marquez said proudly.

Cassidy looked at the monitor. "Prison ward . . . what happens there?"

"We redid everything after the earthquake in '89," said Fayne.

"Spare me the history report, Fayne, would you?" growled Cassidy.

"If the computer crashes or is compromised," Fayne explained, "we switch automatically to a backup at SFPD downtown. That floor stays secure no matter what."

"Get going," said Cassidy. "I want you over there to handle it personally. Got it?"

Fayne got it and went.

chapter 17

Nate wheeled Matt's bed down the corridor. It was lit only by the sweep of the searchlight that moved across the windows from the street. Matt clutched the radio as if it was a lifeline, while Nate babbled about anything that came into his head, trying to keep the kid's mind off the danger he might be in.

He was jabbering about something, some new piece of software he had bought recently, when Matt realized he couldn't stand it anymore.

"Uh . . . Nate?" Matt's eyes were wide with fear. "Let's not talk about this right now, okay?"

Nate nodded. "Sure."

"Any idea where my dad is?" Matt really needed to hear his father's voice. He peered at the radio and keyed it. "Dad? Come in, Dad?"

Frank Connor responded almost immediately. "Matt? What's going on? Where are you?"

"Matt," Nate whispered, "tell him we're—"

"Dad. The lights went out here. Did they go out where you are?"

Frank Connor was on the fourth floor of the building, moving down a dark corridor. "Yeah, they went here too," said Frank, doing his best to keep his voice soft and reassuring. "It was kind of scary, wasn't it?"

Matt's voice came back strong, as if his father had just given him an infusion of courage. "It's not that bad, Dad."

Frank smiled. Despite everything, he loved talking to his son. He was about to reply when he heard the leather click of boots on the corridor and the crackle of radio traffic. It was a SWAT detail. And they had heard him too.

The team advanced quickly, the beams of their flashlights nosing into the darkness. They came around the corner cautiously, guns up, following the sound of the radio. But all they found was the handset propped against an open door. Frank was gone.

Matt's voice continued to burble. "Dad, Nate says to tell you we're moving. Where? . . . Dad . . . Dad? Are you there?"

But Frank wasn't there; he was pounding down the stairs, the SWAT team in hot pursuit. He burst out of the stairwell and ran into the maternity ward. One of the first sections of the hospital to be evacuated, it was eerily quiet. He dove beneath a row of bassinets, holding his breath, waiting until the SWAT team passed by. In a second or two, they had raced down the corridor, their boots ringing on the floor.

Frank allowed himself to breathe again and slowly got to his feet, glancing out the window as he did so. He was looking down on the bridge, the walkway, connecting the new and old buildings of the hospital complex. Nate was pushing Matt's bed across the span, making for the old building. Frank reached for the radio he usually carried, but realized that he had left it behind on the upper story. Then he froze. On the roof of the walkway, above Matt and Nate, was McCabe, the canvas bag full of cyclopropane tanks slung on his back as if he were some kind of criminal Santa Claus.

Nate and Matt did not know that McCabe was so close, and neither did the guards on the walkway. They blocked the entrance to the old building.

Nate flashed his badge. "I'm taking this boy to the isolation ward—sixth floor."

One of the guards shook his head. "We got orders. No one gets through."

Nate nodded and looked as if he understood their predicament. "Okay . . . okay. . . . Thing is, though, the kid just got back from Africa. They think he's got that, what's it called . . . Ebola. Look—I'm just going to leave him here while I—"

"Okay, okay," said the other guard. "We get the point."

Both of the men got out of the way so fast that even Matt smiled.

There was a security barrier on the old building end of the walkway, a tall coil of razor wire. McCabe set down the cyclopropane tanks, carefully placing them in the gutter, then throwing the canvas bag over the wire. He hoisted himself up and crawled over the knifelike wire, cutting his hands and knees as he went.

Frank was not the only one who had spotted McCabe. The monitors in the prison ward security booth had picked him up too as he hopped down from the fence and stepped up to the sixth-floor door.

The guard in the security booth grabbed his radio. "There he is!" he yelled. "I've got the suspect on top of the walkway!"

Cassidy's voice came back immediately. "Keep him in sight," he ordered.

The SWAT commander was issuing orders of his own. "Give me a sierra team on that spot right now."

The infectious diseases lab was protected by a thick metal door leading to a secure air lock. Nate punched the code into the electronic lock and the door swung open noiselessly.

But the noise inside the lab was terrifying. As soon as Nate wheeled the bed into the laboratory the air was split with a terrifying screeching sound. Both Matt and Nate jumped about a foot.

Behind a glass partition they could see a dozen or more monkeys in cages, all of them screaming at the sight of two humans. Even without the monkeys, the place was not inviting. The walls were lined with vials and tubes containing mysterious cultures and strains of viruses; biohazard signs seemed to be stuck on every surface. On a control panel a single button was marked: "Emergency quarantine—Do not press—Lab lockdown."

"Whatever comes in here they don't want to let out," Nate said, giving in to a rare failure of nerve.

McCabe was nothing more than a shadow on the wall, impossible to get a good fix on until the searchlight mounted on the SWAT team armored car came on. The beam transfixed him against the red brick, throwing him into a circle of light as if he were about to sing an aria. McCabe could see nothing, but he knew what was out there. He could feel the imminence of death and he twisted left and right, making himself a moving target. But he knew they could not miss, not these guys. . . .

The first two shots went wide, one to the left, one to the right, as if they were fixing him, estimating the distance to target. The third round nicked him—ironically catching him in the hip, the one Samantha Hawkins had been prepared to work on many hours earlier. He knew the next shot would kill him. . . . He closed his eyes and smiled: Well, he had tried. . . .

Then there was a shot, the sound of shattering glass—and the searchlight died with a hiss. McCabe opened his eyes. It was night. It was dark and he was still alive. He could see Frank Connor standing in the shattered window of the maternity ward, his gun in his hand.

McCabe cackled as the realization hit him: Frank Connor had shot out the searchlight. McCabe's face lit up like a kid's.

"Frank!" he shouted. "My man!"

chapter 18

The radio chatter was frantic.

"What happened?" the SWAT commander wanted to know.

"Someone shot out the light."

"Who the hell did that?"

Jerry Cassidy was mad enough to punch the wall. "Shit!" he shouted. He knew exactly who had shot out the light.

The SWAT team that had been searching for Frank was coming back and he heard them. He knew he couldn't make it down the hall. They would be on him in a second if he tried to escape that way. He looked out the window. It was a sheer drop to the ground. He looked up and saw two ropes dangling from a window washer's scaffold. It was the only way to go.

A searchlight split the night once again and focused on McCabe's last position—no McCabe. The beam swung around to the maternity ward and a bullet was right behind, it blowing out another window.

Frank had caught the scaffold rope and he hauled himself up, hand over hand, until he was lying flat on the platform. Beneath him he could hear the SWAT team tearing apart the maternity ward looking for any sign of him, then, to his relief, he heard the team leader calling in a negative.

Besides, there were more important—and lethal—developments taking place. The searchlight had spotted something else—an open window on the sixth floor, the floor that housed the prison ward.

"The suspect went in on the sixth floor of the old building," someone announced over a radio. "Repeat: He is on the sixth floor."

Cassidy knew what was going on at once. "He's going to the prison ward. He'll try to start a riot." He grabbed his radio. "He's on the sixth floor. Tell Warden Fayne to have his men cut off stairwells and elevators for everything above five."

Fayne got the order immediately. "McCabe entered the building on the sixth floor," he told his guards. "Distribute weapons and go and find him."

Two guards unlocked the weapons closet and started handing out automatic weapons. They checked the magazines then started for the stairs.

Frank was still on the scaffold, but like a fly on the wall he could get a sense of everything that was going on around him. He could hear prison guards all over the building, shouts and curses echoing as guards ran into SWAT teamers and almost blew each other away. He could see Fayne in his control center talking to his men as they radioed in with the increasingly bad news.

"We can't find him on five or six."

Fayne grimaced when he heard this. "Leave two men there and bring the rest back." He was staring at the radio as if he could see what was happening on the other floors. He did not notice a shadow gliding up behind him—suddenly he had a hypodermic needle at his throat. A bolt of fear like hot lead seemed to burn its way through his body.

"This thing is full of sulfuric acid," McCabe whispered into Fayne's ear. "Do you know how ugly and horrible this will make you? You'll look like your own soul."

Fayne quelled his fear enough to say: "What's your soul look like, McCabe?"

McCabe smiled, as if pleased that Fayne had found the wherewithal to be defiant. "My soul? No one's ever seen it."

When the guards returned to the prison ward security station they were greeted by the sight of McCabe and the warden still locked in their strange little embrace, the hypodermic still poised at Fayne's fleshy neck.

McCabe smiled, as if welcoming them back. "I suggest everyone listen very carefully. Anybody who doesn't like the boss, make a move and I will inject the warden—two seconds later, his nervous system will stop operating. His stomach will discharge through his mouth. His heart will stop beating and he will die on the floor in a pool of his own vomit.'' McCabe said this with the definite suggestion that he would not have minded seeing this, as if it would be sort of interesting, like something on public television.

Fayne was sweating profusely and trying to fight the panic churning through him. The guards listened and gulped.

''So,'' McCabe continued, ''please bring your weapons to the control booth on behalf of this poor man. And I want the prisoners to lock all the guards in the day room. Now open the sally ports. . . .''

The electric gates slid open with a grinding of gears. McCabe pushed Fayne through the open gates and into the control booth, the needle never leaving Fayne's neck.

All the weapons were collected in an orderly fashion and locked in the security booth. The guards were locked in the day room and the prisoners were in control, patrolling the hallways.

McCabe grabbed a set of handcuffs and forced Fayne to the floor, cuffing one ankle to the steel leg of the computer console. Then McCabe sat down at the computer console and cracked his knuckles, like a concert pianist about to play a particularly complicated piece. He put out a hand to Fayne.

''Your computer card, please, Warden.''

Fayne did not move, so McCabe jabbed a millimeter or so of the needle into the man's flesh. The warden gasped and grimaced, but McCabe did not inject . . . yet.

''Shirt . . . pocket,'' Fayne gasped.

McCabe reached down into the breast pocket of Fayne's short-sleeved shirt and pulled out a magnetic-faced card hanging by a metal chain from Fayne's neck. He yanked the chain, breaking it, and inserted the card into the computer's A drive. Instantly the monitor asked for a password. McCabe did not ask Fayne for it. Rather, he just put his thumb on the plunger of the hypodermic needle.

Fayne got the message right away. "Firefly," he said, his voice hoarse. "All it lets me do is run the lights and the cell doors."

McCabe chuckled. "That's all it lets *you* do, Warden. Let's see what it'll do for me, shall we?"

McCabe's fingers flew over the keys with assurance, but each gambit resulted in a single prompt: NO ACCESS PERMITTED.

"Well," said McCabe. "That's not good enough. Let's try something else. . . ."

Whatever the something else was it seemed to work. Fayne's eyes grew wide as the computer began to respond. A table of "authorities" clicked on, filling the screen—the names and personal passwords of everyone allowed on the computers . . . including their levels of access. McCabe scrolled down to the highest authority, the one with total access. With a little smile on his face he typed in that word.

Samantha Hawkins had to get to Matt. She was in the new building, her patient was in the old. In between were any number of policemen, security guards, and, as far as she knew, prison guards. Not to mention an extremely dangerous criminal with nothing to lose.

But she was determined to cross that walkway, even if she had to cross it the way McCabe had—

on the roof. The trouble was, she was deathly afraid of heights.

Frank Connor had to get on to that walkway too, but luckily he had no fear of heights. He loosened one of the ropes on the scaffolding platform until it hung free, the boards tilting unsteadily under his feet. He took a deep breath and kicked off the platform, swinging out into the void.

At the widest arc of the swing he was almost directly over the walkway roof. He threw himself forward, letting go of the rope and landing with a thud on the walkway roof. But the roof was slick and slippery and Frank slid toward the edge, grabbing at the gutter an instant before he fell the five stories to the pavement. He swung there a moment, then hoisted himself up onto the roof and lay flat, breathing deeply, before slowly getting to his feet.

Then Frank turned and saw Samantha Hawkins climbing out onto the walkway, shimmying through a window in the new building. Frank grabbed her and dragged her down.

"What the hell are you doing?" he whispered frantically.

"Matt is over there," she said. "He needs me." She had a medical bag slung over her shoulder.

"Tell me what to do," said Frank. "I'll do it. Give me the bag."

Hawkins held on to the bag. "It took me four years in med school, an internship, a residency, and five years on staff here to know what to do. Do we have that long, Frank?"

"No. You're right." Then he noticed that Hawkins was trembling, her knees had locked, and her body was rigid.

"You okay?"

"I'm sorry. . . ." She kicked off her shoes and then tried to get up again, but her body would not respond to the orders she was giving it.

"Problem with heights?" Frank asked.

Samantha nodded miserably and looked sick to her stomach.

"This is not a great time to find out about it," he said.

"I'm not finding out," she replied. "I always knew I had it."

"Give me your hand," he said, reaching toward her. Samantha wanted to take it, but was afraid to. She waved him away and forced herself to take a step. Then she sat down again.

"You go ahead."

"Don't be—"

"No, please, go ahead. I need to be . . . Just go. Don't look back. Don't look at me."

Frank went, but he went slowly, forcing himself not to look back. As he went Samantha rose to her feet again, but her legs continued to tremble and she sat again, burying her face on her upraised knees.

In the police command center, Cassidy and Marquez stared at a computer just like the one across the way in the prison ward. They were, of course, completely unaware of Hawkins's dilemma.

"We can override his lockout," Marquez said. "That terminal has limited authority. I can unlock it at anytime, and your men can move in."

"Don't talk about it," said Cassidy. "Do it."

chapter 19

McCabe was playing with his new toy, the computer that controlled everything—every door, every window, every elevator, every lock—in the entire building. All around the building, doors locked and unlocked, lights click on and off, gates like medieval portcullises descended and raised, bars snapped closed over the door to the top of the walkway.

McCabe was delighted. "Give me a lever and a place to stand . . ." The prisoners watching him missed the classical allusion.

Then he discovered, to his delight, that he could control the video monitors scattered around the building.

"I am in charge here. . . ." The prisoners missed his reference to General Al Haig as well.

McCabe grabbed a radio. "All you boys walking around in the tier . . . you have one minute to get yourselves to the fifth-floor day room or I will start killing your buddies."

There was a loud, throaty roar of approval from the prisoners on the ward. McCabe hit a couple of buttons, activated a camera, and zoomed in on a guard on the sixth floor.

"You hear that—fat boy scratching your ass on the sixth floor?"

The beefy guard whirled around and stared at the camera. Then he and the rest of the guards Fayne had scattered around the building started heading for the fifth-floor day room.

Next, McCabe hit the switches that controlled the doors separating the infectious disease ward from the lab. Matt and Nate gaped as doors started to open.

Samantha Hawkins had not moved. Frank was on the far side of the walkway roof—but he had still not looked back. Finally, she breathed deep and decided that enough was enough. She stood up and started to walk as if she were out for a stroll on a summer afternoon.

She slipped, but she fought to get her footing in an instant and she walked on, fighting her fear. Frank still hadn't looked back, but he could tell she was coming and he reached behind, holding his hand out. This time she seized it and held it tight.

It was up to the SWAT team now. Cassidy went to the SWAT commander and put his cards on the table.

"We don't know what the hell he's done with the

computer over there,'' he said. ''If we can shut him down can you get a man in there?''

''We're working on it.''

Marquez was still at the console. ''I'm switching to the backup computer downtown at SFPD,'' he said with a grin. ''It'll freeze him out.''

''Good,'' said Cassidy, smiling for the first time in a day. ''Let's go!''

But McCabe was a step ahead of them. The changeover had been recorded and overridden on the computer in the prison ward.

McCabe cackled. ''Every time they close one door they open another.'' His fingers flew across the keyboard and in an instant a message was appearing on Marquez's screen. Over and over again it read: EAT SHIT AND DIE EAT SHIT AND DIE EAT SHIT AND DIE . . .

''What the hell is that?'' Cassidy demanded, the smile gone now.

''It's a message—from him.''

''What does it mean?''

''It means that somehow he's got control of the SFPD backup. How the hell did he do that?'' Marquez felt sick to his stomach.

The bitter truth was sinking in on Cassidy. ''He's a piece of trailer trash who reads. He's smart. Smarter than you, me, and maybe Bill Gates. And he's got us where he wants us.''

''He's controlling the automatic systems in the old building, but the hospital is surrounded,'' said Marquez. ''There's no way he can escape.''

Cassidy whipped around and faced the SWAT commander. ''So how do we get in there?''

"We could go with explosives," the man said. "But he's got all the guards and all the prisoners as hostages. We can move fast, but not fast enough to save them all." It was a simple statement of fact: Some of the hostages would die if McCabe was attacked.

"But there must be a fail-safe," Cassidy protested. "There's *gotta* be."

Marquez watched EAT SHIT AND DIE continue to scroll across the screen. "The fail-safe was not letting him escape in the first place."

McCabe had noticed Frank and Samantha on the roof of the walkway. They were approaching the barrier that blocked the entrance to the old building.

There was a great roar out of the night sky as a chopper swooped down and hovered just above the walkway, the wash of the blades all but sweeping them from the roof. They flattened themselves on the roof and blocked their ears against the awful noise. A blinding light dropped from the chopper and caught them in the beam.

"This is a restricted area!" The voice came over a loudspeaker. "Move inside the building at once."

Frank cupped his hands around his mouth. "Get back, we're going to fall!"

"Move inside the building!"

Frank and Samantha remained in a crouch, inching forward, but the chopper bobbed about just above their heads, buffeting them with the wash. Hidden in the cab of the chopper was a man with a sniper's rifle. Frank couldn't believe they would send out a shooter for them—they could have been picked off from any point on the hospital roof. Then it dawned on him. This was a diversion—they were trying to insert a single gunman into the old building.

McCabe watched this little drama play out on the monitor, engrossed. He had not seen the sniper, of course, but it was fascinating nonetheless. Without taking his eyes off the screen he picked up the radio at his elbow.

"Get me Cassidy."

Marquez received the transmission and handed the radio to his superior. "It's McCabe. He wants you."

"This is Cassidy."

"I know who it is," McCabe snapped. "Now, listen to me, you—"

"No," Cassidy yelled back. "You listen to me. I want you to—"

McCabe shrugged and clicked off the radio. He looked at some of the prisoners who were watching his every move. "What can you do with someone like that?"

Cassidy couldn't quite believe that he had been cut off. He was still holding the radio to his ear when it came to life again. There was a long pause before McCabe deigned to speak.

"Are you ready to listen?"

Cassidy gritted his teeth, but he was ready to listen. "Go ahead."

"What is going on with that chopper?" McCabe asked.

"We are trying to get Connor and Dr. Hawkins off the roof."

"Well, get that thing out of here. Now. Or I'll kill Fayne."

Fayne was lying on the floor, curled at McCabe's feet, the hypodermic dangling from a little cut in his neck. McCabe reached down and put his thumb on the plunger. With the other hand he held the radio to the unfortunate man's mouth. The warden did not need any more prompting.

He was breathless with terror. "Do what he says. Please. . . ."

Cassidy could not decide how to play this. He was indifferent to what happened to Fayne, but Cassidy knew he could not carry the weight of a dozen hostages. Finally he said, "Okay, we'll get the chopper out of there." He clicked the radio dead and turned to the SWAT commander. "Try one more pass to drop your man, but for Chrissakes, hurry up."

The SWAT commander grabbed his own radio. "You got one more shot at it. Now."

The helicopter made one last low pass over the roof, the rotors blowing up a cloud of dust and debris that obscured the lens of the security camera for just long enough for the SWAT officer to drop a rope over the side and slide down to the security camera. With lightning expertise he attached alligator clips to the camera wires and jammed the lead into the port of a miniature cassette player showing a continuous loop of an empty roof.

With a roar, the chopper lifted off and all McCabe could see was a sweep of the empty roof.

"Excellent," said McCabe. "Thank you. Now, I have one further demand. Listen and do not speak. I want a six-seat helicopter with a range of two hundred miles fully fueled, on the roof in fifteen minutes. It will have one pilot and when he lands he will open the doors so I can see inside. And there will be no firepower within line of sight. Understood?"

Cassidy answered, "Understood."

"I will board the helicopter within two minutes of landing," McCabe continued. "If that does not take place within sixteen minutes from right now, I will start killing hostages at five-minute intervals."

Cassidy, Marquez, and the SWAT commander listened to McCabe's voice, hating every word.

"There will be no further negotiations," said McCabe tersely. "And there will be no attempt to contact me. Over and out." There was a click and the radio went dead. All eyes were on Cassidy.

"Go on," he said. "Get him his chopper." Marquez and the SWAT commander looked surprised.

"You serious?" Marquez yelled.

"How long before your man gets in there?" Cassidy asked the SWAT commander.

The commander shrugged. "He's got to cut blockers in the vents—but he might make it in fifteen. We have a team ready for direct assault. We'll put snipers he can't see on surrounding rooftops. And if it comes down to it, we'll have an extra man in the copter. . . . There is no way out for him."

On the roof of the prison ward the SWAT team member who had disabled the camera was now using a tiny, superhot blowtorch to silently cut a hole in the vents leading down into the building. Once the first bar came away, he slid himself into the air hole, and slid away into the darkness.

chapter 20

McCabe was watching the roof as if he were watching a movie, staring as Frank and Hawkins slowly made their way into the prison building.

"Go, Frank," said McCabe, as if urging on a sports team. "Everybody watch this," McCabe ordered the prisoners. "Now, you see that? A lesson for you all. That man has a goal and damned if he's not determined to achieve it. You gotta respect that. I was skeptical at first, but now, you know, I really do think he loves that kid of his. . . ." Peter McCabe felt envious. He could not recall having felt that before.

The voice of the SWAT commander barely whispered in the ear of his man working his way inside.

"Talk to me."

"Here."

"How long?"

"Ten minutes."

The SWAT commander clicked off the radio. He turned to Cassidy. "He won't be in position for at least ten minutes."

Cassidy nodded. "That's doable."

"And when the chopper comes down, McCabe will move to the roof. We'll have snipers waiting."

Frank had sliced his hand open on the razor wire. Hawkins grabbed it and looked at it.

"That's not good."

"I want you to sew me up later," said Frank, wincing with the pain.

"Sure. Of course."

Frank did his best to smile. "Not some nurse," he said. "You."

Samantha understood that he was saying a lot more than a request for medical attention. Samantha nodded. "Okay. Of course."

The SWAT scout had worked his way down through the building until he hit the ventilation grate in the ceiling of the floor above the prison ward. He slipped a fiber-optic probe out of one of the pockets in his jumpsuit and slid it through a slit in the grate. He pulled the mouthpiece of his headset close to his mouth.

"I'm there," he whispered. He peered through the eyepiece of the probe, scanning the prison security booth beneath him. It was empty. "But he's not."

The fiber-optic tube pivoted, looking for McCabe. As the wire turned it disturbed some grit from the tile joins in the ceiling, the dust drifting down like black snow. Then the probe stopped moving. It had found what it was looking for.

McCabe was leading Fayne across the hall to the day room.

"Time to go to the roof." McCabe pointed to three guards. "You, you, and you come with me."

None of the guards looked very happy about being chosen by McCabe. "I thought it was going to be fifteen minutes. I heard you say fifteen minutes."

McCabe nodded and looked sort of patient. "You're right. I said fifteen minutes. But we're going up now. Okay?"

The radio squawked. "McCabe. It's Frank Connor. I need to talk to you."

All over the hospital complex, cops were picking up this transmission.

"What the hell is he doing now?" Cassidy yelled. He grabbed his own radio and bellowed into the mouthpiece. "Get Connor back in here!"

Even McCabe seemed surprised to hear from Frank. "No one is supposed to contact me, Frank. I guess you didn't hear. I suppose you've been out of the loop a little. Nobody's fault. . . ."

At that moment three SWAT officers were climbing out onto the walkway. No one saw them.

Frank steadied Samantha with one hand while holding the radio with the other. "McCabe, listen, Matt needs medical attention right away—"

McCabe's voice came back clear as a bell. Samantha and Frank could hear the chuckle in his voice. "And I need a hard drink and an easy woman—I guess we'll both have to wait."

Frank didn't laugh. "He's in your building. He's in the infectious disease lab. Let his doctor see him. You don't care about him but—"

"Oh, I care," said McCabe quickly. "I know his doctor. Dr. Hawkins. Had I but world enough and time . . ."—Frank missed the quote from Andrew Marvell—"He can see her in fifteen minutes, if your friends do as I say. And, really, I do care."

"Look, it's about your freedom," said Frank urgently. "You want out—"

"I told you once, Frank, do not try to get inside my head."

"What do you think I'd find there? It couldn't be worse than what you've done already."

McCabe started to respond, then stopped himself. Instead, he steered the handcuffed men out of the day room and into the hallway. The prisoners backed off as the little procession passed, giving McCabe a wide and respectful berth.

"I can help you, McCabe," said Frank.

But McCabe knew a hustle when he heard it. He took the hostages into the security booth of the prison and looked at the monitors.

"Sure, Frank, you'd help me. . . ."

The SWAT officer in the vent saw McCabe clearly with the fiber-optic probe. Silently he chambered a bullet into his automatic.

"So tell me," said McCabe. "What would you do for me?"

"What if I've done my homework?" Frank said. "What if I know everything you know?"

McCabe thought about this for a moment, his eyes on the tiled floor. There was a pile of black dust at his feet. He did not remember having seen that before.

"McCabe?" said Frank. "You there?"

"Yeah," McCabe replied. He sounded a little preoccupied. "Just a second, Frank, okay?" He sounded like an executive putting a caller on hold. McCabe looked up and saw the short neck of the optic probe snaking out of the vent. McCabe did not hesitate. He yanked his gun out of his pocket and fired four times into the ceiling. The shots were placed very neatly.

Frank heard the shots. "What was that?"

"Just a rat," said McCabe casually. "I shot a rat. That's all."

Blood was dripping out of the holes in the ceiling.

"So what were you saying, Frank? You've done your homework? Very good. What did you learn?"

"Everything you learned when you did your homework," said Frank. "I learned the lay of the land. Down to the last drop."

For the first time all night McCabe showed some concern. "How many of us share this information?"

"Just you and me," said Frank. "For now, that is. We can keep it that way if you open the door."

Cassidy, Marquez, and the SWAT commander were listening to this as if they were following an old-fashioned radio serial.

"Connor is selling us out," said Cassidy. "That son of a bitch."

McCabe's voice was soft and questioning. "Can I trust you, Frank?"

Cassidy turned to the SWAT commander, his face a mask of hatred. "I want you to get Connor. Get him now."

chapter 21

Frank Connor realized he was in a place he had never been before, someplace he was not welcome, someplace he had never expected to be. Finally, he was inside the head of Peter McCabe.

"I don't know," he whispered into the microphone like a teasing lover. "Can you trust me?" He and Samantha had finally crawled into the building only to be confronted with a locked gate, a gate that only McCabe could control. But Frank knew that it would be opened for him, if only he could continue.

Suddenly, it was McCabe's capacities that were in doubt, not Frank's.

The moment of euphoria lasted for a moment, no longer. Then the cold, blunt nose of a Heckler and Koch machine pistol poked into his ear.

"Put down the radio and stand up," a SWAT member whispered. "You are both under arrest. . . ."

It was almost as if McCabe didn't need a radio to know that something had gone awry. "What's going on?" McCabe's voice crackled through the radio. "Who's there?"

There was no answer from Frank. Nothing came out of the radio except static.

"Cassidy! Pick up right now!" McCabe ordered. His voice almost broke as he spoke.

"I'm here," said Cassidy.

"Your dogs are doing something to Connor," said McCabe passionately. "What is it? *What are they doing to my friend?*"

Cassidy's voice was slick and sarcastic. "Your *friend* is being arrested." McCabe could almost see Cassidy doing the quote sign with his fingers as he said that word—friend.

"No, he is not," McCabe replied. He looked down at his control board and hit a single switch. Instantly the gate blocking the progress of Frank and Samantha rose. They now had access to the old building.

McCabe's voice came over the radio, warm and welcoming. "Come on in, Frank."

The guy with the H&K in Frank's ear shook his head. "Don't move or we'll shoot."

McCabe knew exactly what was going on. "Cassidy, I want those cops out of there."

"This has nothing to do with you," Cassidy responded. He looked at Marquez and the SWAT commander. They all knew it was a lame thing to say, but he had to say *something*.

McCabe was particularly annoyed by the response. "Do not tell me what has to do with me, you stupid fuck. I decide what has to do with me. I decide.'' He reached out and grabbed the prison guard closest to him. The guard's name was stenciled on his chest: Wachtler.

''I'm going to kill Wachtler now, just to show you. Okay?''

''No,'' said Wachtler.

Without hesitation, McCabe raised his gun and pulled the trigger, firing a single shot.

The gunshot could be heard across the yard, through the radio. It seemed to echo everywhere.

''Now,'' said McCabe. ''I want you to get your fucking men away from Connor right now. Or Fayne is next. Everybody clear on that?''

Cassidy was not a happy man. He put the radio to his lips. ''Team C, copy?''

''Team C,'' replied the guy with the H&K machine pistol.

''Do not touch Connor.''

McCabe watched the SWAT guy withdraw. Wachtler was still standing there, unharmed.

''What a pussy that Cassidy is,'' said McCabe, laughing out loud. ''The guards at Pelican Bay would never have gone for that shit.''

The prisoners in the hall roared their approval, although a number of them would have preferred to see McCabe actually kill a screw.

''Bravo,'' McCabe crowed. ''And, uh, withdraw. . . . Leave him. No surveillance. Remember, I see everything.''

Cassidy's voice was clipped. ''Team C—follow the directive.''

''Good. Now. You have eight minutes left to bring

me my helicopter. Without that, they will become the dead. Understand?''

The SWAT team dropped their weapons and backed off. They looked slightly sick. Frank Connor wanted to say something, to tell them that there was a plan, that he hadn't gone over to the other side. But right then he didn't dare to say any more.

Onward. Frank and Samantha started toward the open gate—but then Frank stopped, noticing the tank of cyclopropane that had been left in the gutter.

''Frank?'' McCabe's voice sounded amused again. ''Are you there?''

''I'm still here.''

''You're noticing my gratuity, I see?''

Frank looked from the tank to the camera lens bolted on the tower wall. He stared right into the lens. His face was huge in McCabe's monitor.

''You don't need to kill anyone else,'' Frank said quietly.

''In a situation such as this,'' said McCabe airily, ''credibility is everything. Do you agree?''

''You have your credibility, McCabe. Look at what's going on around here tonight. They could not possibly be taking you more seriously. Neither could I.''

''We're a team now, Frank,'' said McCabe. ''Do you agree?''

Frank shook his head. ''We're not a team.'' He looked into the monitor and appeared to be genuinely contrite. ''We are *not* a team.''

McCabe turned his attention back to his computer keyboard. ''Frankie . . . we've been a team since I met you. Don't delude yourself. You showed your teamwork back there in the emergency room. I thank you for that.'' McCabe laughed and shook his head. ''In fact, I thank you for everything.''

Frank and Samantha were standing just inside the gate. It was time to check in with Matt and Nate.

''Nate? You read me? How is Matt?''

Nate's voice came back immediately. ''Frank! Where the hell are you?''

''Hawkins is on her way up,'' Frank replied. ''I'll catch up with her.''

He nodded at the doctor. She started into the building, but Frank stopped her. He had not lost sight of the ultimate goal. ''If we had to, could we transplant the bone marrow up in the isolation ward?''

Hawkins thought about it for a moment. ''Yes,'' she said. ''They have syringes, anesthetic . . . I don't see why not.''

McCabe knew it was time to move. He shoved Fayne and the other hostages toward the door, but they sort of bounced around, unable to adjust to the handcuffs that bound them all together.

''You daisy chain boys,'' said McCabe, ''you just follow me.''

McCabe turned back and faced the remaining prisoners and guards. ''In about ten seconds, the gates are going to open. Do not try to follow. Also, do not touch the computer board or the radio. If you do, the whole thing will fry. Sit back, relax, think about the meaning of life. Try to focus on your futures, what you hope to accomplish. Okay?''

The guards and the prisoners looked at him doubtfully, as if he was speaking in an unfathomable foreign language, like French.

"Understand?"

The guards and prisoners mumbled okay.

"That's the spirit."

A message flashed on the computer screen in the police command post. It read: THANKS FOR A PLEASURABLE STAY AND FOR PUTTING UP WITH MY ECCENTRICITIES. SORRY ABOUT THE MESS.

Cassidy, Marquez, and the SWAT commander read it and then looked at each other.

"That's it," Cassidy pronounced. "He's moving."

"So are we," said the SWAT commander.

chapter 22

McCabe marched his handcuffed foursome toward the roof, but just shy of the top floor he stopped them on the stairs. He had intended to leave them a few feet behind him on the stairs while he took a peek out onto the roof to see if the chopper he had ordered was anywhere in sight.

But before he got to the door he looked out the window flanking the staircase and saw Cassidy and a bunch of SWATs creeping across the roof of the walkway. They had not seen the canisters of cyclopropane wedged in the gutters, but Frank had.

Connor punched the key on his radio. ''Cassidy, come in. Cassidy?''

Cassidy and the SWAT team stopped on the bridge as Frank's call came in. Cassidy grabbed the radio.

''Get off this frequency, Connor!'' In one short

night, Jerry Cassidy had had enough of Frank Connor to last a lifetime or two.

But Connor didn't care what Cassidy thought of him. "Cassidy—do not send your men! Repeat! Do *not!*"

The SWAT commander's voice broke in, ruining Frank's transmission. "That bastard is giving the whole thing away."

The opposite was true. Frank Connor was trying to warn the SWAT guys and the rest of them, but all of his messages were broken up or stepped on.

"There's a canister on the—"

Cassidy hit the button on his radio. "I've lost you, Connor. Completely." He clicked off the radio and turned to the commander of the SWAT unit. "Let's go."

Only Frank Connor and Peter McCabe knew that the bridge was going to be blown up. Only Frank Connor cared. He unholstered his gun, aimed carefully, and fired, blowing out a window on the walkway.

"Christ!" the SWAT commander shouted. "It's Connor. He's shooting at us!" The entire team fell back, withdrawing to the safety of the new hospital building, leaving the air bridge open to attack.

Frank squeezed off another carefully placed shot, then another, pushing the cops back even further into the main building.

Then the tank of cyclopropane exploded in a vast fiery ball, immediately followed by secondary explosions from gas lines and electrical boxes. Orange flames were shooting in every direction.

The explosion was too much for the air bridge.

Metal twisted and strained under the onslaught of the explosions, then finally gave way. A great flaming ball of wreckage tumbled five stories to the ground.

After all Cassidy had gone through that night he never imagined that he would end up absolutely dumbfounded. But he was now. "Connor . . . he blew the thing up," said Cassidy. "He is fucking helping McCabe. He could have killed us all."

The SWAT commander saw it differently. He knew that Connor had not caused the explosions. He had fired a couple of shots, but he hadn't detonated the cyclopropane. One thing he was sure of: If the team had been on that bridge when it exploded they would all be dead now. He turned to Cassidy. "*You* think he tried to kill us. But actually he saved our lives."

It took another three precious minutes for the chopper to lift off, a sharpshooter crouched behind one of the seats. Just as the machine was about to pull up and leave the ground, Cassidy dove into the cabin and did his best to hide himself.

"Now!" he screamed. "Go!"

The helicopter rose into the air and traveled the few hundred feet to the roof in a matter of seconds. A group of hostages was waiting there . . . but no McCabe.

Frank didn't give a damn anymore. All he wanted to do was get to his son. As he walked toward the ward where his son was hidden he raised the radio to his lips.

"Nate, I'm here. It's me, Frank."

"Thank God." Nate sounded genuinely relieved. The door of the ward began to open but before Frank could reach it McCabe stepped out of the shadows and into his path, blocking Frank's way.

Frank did not hesitate. "Nate! Close the door! McCabe is there! Close it now!"

Nate hit the emergency close button and the door rolled shut, airtight.

McCabe and Connor were stuck on the outside face to face.

"Teamwork, Frank. Tell your friend to open it up."

Frank did nothing. He did not move. He did not speak. McCabe swore quietly then hit the intercom on the wall.

"This is Peter McCabe. Acknowledge, please."

"Nate!" Frank shouted. "Don't!"

McCabe sighed and leveled the gun at Frank's head. Once again he hit the intercom button. "Nate, listen to me. I cannot be killed. I am immortal, thanks to my kinship with Matt. Frank, on the other hand, will be dead in ten seconds if you do not open this fucking door right now! Hear me, Nate?"

"Don't do it!" Frank yelled.

Inside the lab Nate could not decide what to do. Matt knew exactly what had to be done. He slammed his fist into the button and the door pulled open.

"Come on, Frank," said McCabe wearily. "Let's go."

Killer and cop walked into the infectious disease lab. Matt was lying in his bed, with Nate at the head of his bed and Samantha Hawkins at his side, drawing a syringe of blood from the boy.

Matt smiled when he saw Frank. "Dad . . ." Frank ran to his son and hugged him close.

A flicker of sympathy showed in McCabe's eyes. "Hey, Matt . . ."

Samantha was preparing another needle, as if to draw another specimen from her patient, but suddenly she turned and jammed the syringe through McCabe's sleeve and hit the plunger hard. McCabe reacted instantly, backhanding Hawkins so hard she flew across the room. Nate tried to get him, but McCabe was too fast. He turned and fired twice, both bullets slamming into Nate's gut.

Nate fell to the ground, writhing in pain, holding his stomach. Samantha dropped to her feet and tried to look at the wounds but she did not need to see them to see how serious they were.

There were tears in her eyes. "People keep getting hurt around you."

McCabe was indignant. "If they'd just fucking do what I told them, it wouldn't happen!"

He sounded aggrieved and terribly put out, but he couldn't help glancing at Matt to see what the boy's reaction was to all this. Matt looked back at him with an even, dispassionate gaze that bothered McCabe. Who, he wondered, was this damn little kid who had the guts to stare at him like that.

Frank slipped an arm around Matt's shoulder, but McCabe glanced away, as if embarrassed by the sight.

"Aren't you supposed to be on the roof?" Frank asked. "You know, the helicopter?"

"For losers, Frank. That's for losers. I wouldn't have gotten three feet away in that thing." He looked to Hawkins. "Where's the elevator to the morgue? And let's skip the part where you say 'What elevator?' "

Hawkins cocked her head away from the door. "It's in the back."

The elevator was an old, slow one. It seemed to take forever to arrive and the four people gathered in front of the door had that same self-conscious awkwardness that people always had about waiting for the elevator. No one knew where to look, no one knew what to say.

Except Frank.

"You're going through the tunnels, aren't you?" he said. "Cassidy knows about them."

McCabe shook his head. "No way. No. He's not that smart."

"I told him," said Frank.

"You weren't supposed to help him," McCabe protested. "You promised not to do that."

"I lied," said Frank.

McCabe stared at him for a moment. "I don't think so. . . . But in case you did"—he grabbed Matt by the neck and pulled him close—"my buddy here will come in very handy."

Frank started to lunge, but McCabe jammed the gun into Matt's temple. "Want to test my resolve, Frank? My willingness to go to the limit?" McCabe was trembling with a sudden fury. "Do you want to see where you stop and I begin?"

Frank pulled back as the elevator arrived. Helplessly, he watched as his son and McCabe got into the car. Matt looked back at his father, their eyes never leaving each other's until the door intervened between them.

The elevator descended slowly and the awkwardness returned.

"You know what they used this elevator for?" McCabe asked pedantically. Matt did not reply.

"They used it for dead bodies," said McCabe. "They didn't want to wheel them through the whole hospital. That would only depress everybody, you know. So they had this special elevator that ran straight to the morgue."

McCabe waited for Matt to respond to that jolly little fact. He was disappointed.

"What are you going to do to me?" Matt asked at last.

McCabe shrugged. "I truly don't know."

Matt shrugged too. "It doesn't really matter 'cause I'm going to die anyway."

McCabe, like all the adults, was moved by Matt's display of stoicism. "Your father doesn't think so," he said.

"He can't face it," said Matt simply. It was nothing less than the truth.

The morgue was dark and dank, deserted. They looked around the depressing room. Like the rest of the hospital, the place had been evacuated, but the gruesome tools remained: the autopsy table, the bone saws. In glass cases were heads and other bits and pieces of medical remains.

"How are you feeling?" McCabe asked Matt.

Matt gave him a look and wiped a drop of blood

from his nose. "What do you think, Einstein?"

McCabe was not offended. He laughed out loud. "I like your spirit, you know?"

"Yeah," said Matt. "Great." He looked around the room.

"You don't have to look, you know," said McCabe.

"I want to."

For a moment McCabe was impressed, maybe even a little intimidated. Something pushed him back into his pedantic mode.

"Your dad is right about . . . this cancer business. You can't decide you're going to die. You have to fight. And then you have to keep fighting."

Matt shot him a dirty look. "What for? So I can be sick all the time? Stay inside? Not play with my friends? If I can't have any fun, what's the point?"

McCabe looked at the kid hard. With a few changes, Matt's description of life with cancer could be the same as his own life in prison. The difference was that McCabe was willing to fight, Matt was prepared to die. McCabe, an expert in such matters, realized that Matt was not displaying fear or weakness—rather, he was showing strength, a kind of strength that he had never felt.

"Come on," said McCabe. They walked on together, like father and son, into the land of the dead.

McCabe pulled Matt into an autopsy room just off the main chamber of the morgue. Then he slammed the steel door and bolted it from inside. He smashed a firebox and pulled an ax from the container, then scanned the ceiling until he found a portion of the old masonry where the tiles bulged out unevenly.

"There it is," said McCabe. "There's always a way out." He swung the ax and chopped deep into the rotten tiles until he broke through, revealing an ancient steam main, a duct that had heated the hospital decades before. Matt and McCabe peered into it, but could not see far into the gloom.

McCabe turned to the boy. "This is good-bye. You wait here. They'll come and get you."

Matt said nothing, but did not look disappointed that McCabe was leaving. For his part, McCabe looked quite upset, more moved than he'd have expected and certainly more than he wanted.

"Listen . . . I'm sorry about the . . ." He poked himself in the hip, pressing on the nick he had taken from a sniper's bullet. He had forgotten all about it.

And suddenly he was overcome with an emotion he had never felt—regret. He knew in his soul that he regretted not being able to save Matt and, for a moment, felt half an impulse to give himself up, if only for the kid's sake. The impulse was too strange to find any purchase inside of him and it went against a code he had lived with for too long.

". . . about the transplant. If I could have done it for you . . ." He nodded to himself, as if giving himself absolution to escape, to leave the kid to his fate. "Anyway, you'll do okay."

McCabe turned and started into the steam tunnel. But before he had traveled a foot or two, Matt had grabbed a crowbar from an autopsy table and smacked McCabe with it, hitting the man as hard as he could.

McCabe whipped around. "Ow! Shit!" He rubbed

his back. ''Why did you do that? I didn't do anything to you.''

''My father's gonna get you!'' Matt snarled. ''And when he does, he's gonna kill you!''

For a moment, McCabe looked genuinely hurt. Then he grinned, the smile lighting up his face. ''You know,'' he said, ''we *do* have the same genes, kid.''

''No, we don't,'' said Matt hotly.

McCabe couldn't help but tease him. ''Compatible . . . we're definitely compatible. . . .''

chapter 23

When Frank reached out and grabbed the elevator cable to lower himself down to morgue level, he felt a sharp pain in his hand. He knew he had cut his hand somewhere, someplace, he just couldn't remember where or when. But he paid as little attention as he could to the discomfort and gradually forgot about it as he worked his way down the elevator shaft in search of his son.

The rooms were cold and dark and he hated to think of Matt alone down there. A little bubble of terror broke inside of him as he thought of his boy. "Matt! Where are you?"

"Dad? Dad?"

Matt ran toward the sound of his son's voice, wildly relieved to find him safe and sound where McCabe had left him in the autopsy room.

"You okay?" Frank said as he threw his arms around him.

"Yeah. I guess." Matt pointed to the jagged hole that McCabe had opened with the fire ax. "He went through there."

Frank nodded. Even Matt knew that this night was not yet done. "You go back that way," he said. "Shout. Call out. Dr. Hawkins will find you." He stepped toward the hole, then stopped and looked back at his boy. "Are you going to be okay?"

Matt nodded. "I'll be fine."

McCabe had a head start and he was making good time as he rushed through the tunnel. He had no idea where he was going, but somehow there was a great feeling of happiness in his heart—the very act of escaping, of outwitting the authorities, exhilarated him.

Somewhere ahead of him was the grinding and clanging of machinery. He honed in on it, running through the tunnel.

It was a turbine, an old steel and copper contraption that drove a giant chain, a turn-of-the-century device that McCabe could only gape at for a moment or two until he realized what it was—the mechanism that powered the cable cars. Somehow he had traveled all the way downhill and was under Powell or Van Ness or one of the few streets in the city that still ran the old contrivances.

Cut up, wounded, and exhausted, McCabe still had enough energy to laugh. "Cable cars . . ."

Without hesitation he grabbed one of the cables with his bare hands and held on as it pulled him into the narrow channel, as if he had been swallowed by the wall itself.

Frank arrived just in time to see McCabe's feet disappear into the narrow passage—there was nothing else he could do but follow.

They ran up a steep incline, both men holding on to the raw steel as it pulled them under the streets of the city at twenty miles an hour, whipping them from left to right, following the tracks of the cable cars on the surface.

McCabe's head was spinning and he had lost all sense of direction as the cable pulled him toward the shining bright light of day. He let go of the cable and was spun into a shaft and slammed hard against the wall. Above him was a round iron disk, a manhole set in the middle of some San Francisco street. It was the only way out and McCabe threw himself at it as if he had just woken up from a refreshing night's sleep.

Pulling aside the metal plate, he carefully put it to one side, then stopped, as if he had a better idea. He did not know if he had been followed into the tunnels or not, but he had a feeling he knew how to get rid of any interloper.

Clutching the manhole to his chest, he lowered it into the passage and gave it a push. The circle of steel rolled away into the darkness.

Frank heard it coming and he flattened himself against the wall, narrowly avoiding the heavy iron disk as it wobbled down the passage. He climbed further, pushing himself up the shaft, as if crawling up a mineshaft.

Finally he pulled himself through the manhole. It was dawn and the streets of San Francisco were deserted. Too early for commuters. And no McCabe either.

Through his fatigue and pain, Frank felt a sickening jolt: fear, panic, nausea—to have come this far and then to have lost McCabe in the labyrinth of the city.

He looked around quickly and saw nothing out of the ordinary, no one running, nothing—except for a police cruiser stopped in the middle of the street on the south side of Union Square. A lone cop was standing there, peering at a man prone on the sidewalk. Scattered about were some tools, a couple of lengths of pipe, some metal boxes—just the kinds of things that the guy might have been loading into the trunk of his car until interrupted.

Frank broke into a jog, running toward the cop and the injured man. He flashed his badge at the uniform.

"What happened? Where's his car?"

The cop straightened and looked at him. "Car? What car? I don't know. I just found him lying here like this."

Frank dropped to his knees next to the guy. There was a gash in the side of his head where he had been smacked with something hard.

"Sir? Sir?" Frank yelled at the poor guy. "What kind of car were you driving? What kind of car? What color?"

The injured man tried to speak, but all he could produce was some bloody spittle. He had been hit hard in the mouth as well. Frank did not bother with that, though. He started going through the man's pockets, pulling out a wallet as if he was a thief rolling a drunk.

"Hey!" said the cop. "What are you doing?"

Frank was running for the patrol car. The cop had not even turned off the engine. "I've got his wallet," he shouted over his shoulder. "I'll bring it back. I'm taking your car. You stay with him." Then, as if he thought the young cop might need something to do, he added: "Call an ambulance!"

The cop blinked. "Taking my—"

But Frank was already behind the wheel, speeding off in the black-and-white.

As he raced through the streets he pulled the license from the man's wallet and punched the guy's name and social security number into the computer unit mounted on the dash. In an instant, the screen lit up with information, a full DMV history.

Frank grabbed the microphone from the radio and clicked into the entire traffic patrol net for the city of San Francisco.

"I want an APB on a '91 electric blue Ford pickup," he yelled, reading the information off the screen. "The driver is Peter McCabe. . . ."

chapter 24

McCabe was driving, smoking the last of Samantha Hawkins's cigarettes and singing along with "Proud Mary" on the radio.

"Left a good job in the city, working for the man every night and day . . ." He had many talents. A lovely singing voice was not one of them.

The song was free and Peter McCabe was free with it. The murder and mayhem of the night before were scarcely a memory and the sheer joy of being at liberty had lifted the fatigue and the pain.

"Never did I lose one minute of sleep," he sang, "worryin' 'bout the way things might have been . . ."

All the happiness McCabe had missed in his life and all the happiness he was ever going to get was going to happen now—maybe even this day—or not at all.

Still, whatever happened, he was enjoying these moments. He was a man in a car on a road in America, with a cigarette in his mouth and rock and roll on the radio. Up ahead was the Golden Gate Bridge—to his right was the sweep of San Francisco Bay, to his left the open sea, up ahead the Marin Headlands—it was like driving straight into a commercial.

He drove across the bridge as the song came to an end and he eagerly awaited the next. He took Route 101 off the bridge, straight into Marin, as if he was driving home to Pelican Bay. Then, in his mirror, he saw the SFPD following him, just four cars back.

"San Francisco PD," said McCabe. "What are you doing in Marin, Officer?"

He was doing a safe, law-abiding fifty-five miles per hour, but he decided to get off the highway, flipping on his turn signal. A sickening feeling went through him as he noticed the black-and-white doing just the same thing.

At the bottom of the off ramp, McCabe scanned the rearview mirror as the cop car pulled up, two cars behind the pickup. This time McCabe could make out the face of the driver.

"Frank. . . ." said McCabe, amazed that he had picked up his scent so quickly. Then, instantly, he was furious at having been caught. McCabe slammed the wheel with the heel of his hand. "Get the fuck off my back!"

He jammed his foot down on the accelerator and shot through the intersection, driving fast, with one eye on the mirror.

"Get the fuck off me, Frank!" McCabe screamed. Up ahead there was a bridge. He drove for it, but as he approached, he heard an alarm and iron posts started rising out of the pavement. At first he thought that this was something to do with him, that the cops had sprung some kind of bizarre trap—then he realized that this was an approach to a drawbridge and these iron poles were just meant to stop traffic.

They stopped McCabe. He slammed on the brakes and the pickup skidded to a stop. He leaped out of the truck and started running for the bridge, paying no attention to a bridge keeper who yelled at him to stop. He ran onto the bridge and had to hop up what seemed to be a step in the bridge.

The patrol car swerved to a stop and Frank was running too, weaving through the iron posts, making for the bridge. But the step that McCabe had hopped was now twelve feet high. Frank grabbed a rising girder and started climbing.

McCabe was still running across the bridge—then he stopped, realizing that something was wrong. He was twenty-five feet in the air and rising. Then it hit him—he was on one of those drawbridges whose entire center section lifts straight up. He was marooned on a rectangular piece of steel road one hundred feet in the air.

Peering over the side McCabe tried to decide if he should climb down—then he looked back and was astonished to see Frank Connor walking toward him. McCabe drew and held his handgun, just as Frank held his 9mm. They faced each other like gunfighters in Dodge City, only with Main Street lifted into the clear sky of the early morning.

"That's close enough, Frank."

"Nowhere to go from here—except down."

McCabe looked over Frank's shoulder. "You know . . . I think you have friends."

Frank turned and looked. A helicopter was coming toward them across the water. A sniper in the cabin had his scope fixed on McCabe.

"It's him," he said to Cassidy. "And somebody else."

Cassidy knew who it was without even having to look. "It's Connor. . . . Can you get a shot from up here?"

"Oh yeah," said the sharpshooter. "Try to hold it steady."

Down on the bridge a single round skipped at McCabe's feet. He did not move. But Frank ran at the helicopter, waving his arms frantically.

"Don't! Don't!" he screamed into the sound of the engine. McCabe stepped around him and fired at the chopper, bullets ripping into the Plexiglas nose. Cassidy felt the sting of the broken plastic as it whipped around the cabin.

"Get him!" he ordered.

Frank jumped in front of McCabe just as the sniper fired. The bullet caught Frank in the shoulder and hurled him backward, slamming into McCabe. The two of them fell to the steel plates of the bridge.

McCabe peered up at Frank sprawled across him.

Frank's face was directly above his, but his eyes were closed and his shoulder was a mass of blood. His breath was thick and labored.

"How you doing, Frank?" McCabe asked. "You don't look so good."

"Don't move," Frank said, his voice barely audible. "If you get up they'll shoot you."

"I hear you, but you know what? I got to get out of here." He threw Frank off like a blanket. "Thanks, Frank. You were a big help. Best of luck to you." He ran for the far side of the bridge as Frank rolled over onto his stomach.

"McCabe!" he shouted and fired. The bullet tore into McCabe's left thigh and he dropped. There was pain and shock in his eyes.

"You shot me. . . ." he said in disbelief. "Frank, you *shot* me."

Frank got to his knees and crawled toward McCabe—just as the sniper in the helicopter fixed him in the middle of his scope. Connor did not hear the shot, but he felt something whistle through the air and into McCabe—all the color and life seemed to drain from his face.

Frank watched, speechless, as McCabe tumbled backward, falling to the water below. There was nothing else Frank could do—he jumped right after him.

McCabe hit the water more dead than alive, the blood billowing from the two wounds in his body. He sank like dead weight until Frank reached out and grabbed him by the collar. He managed to pull him back up toward the surface, as if yanking him back from the gates of hell.

Frank dragged McCabe into the shallows of the river and onto the bank.

"Frank," said McCabe, "I'm going. . . ." The entire upper half of his body was covered in blood.

"No," said Frank. "You are not going, McCabe."

"Sorry, Frank. I just don't think I—"

"Yes you will," Frank shouted. "*Yes, you fucking will!*" He grabbed McCabe's hand. "You are going to live. You're gonna live as long as it takes. Am I right? Am I right, Pete?"

He was squeezing McCabe's hand as if to impart his own will through the skin. McCabe's hand closed around Frank's and squeezed back.

They got McCabe to an operating room alive. Samantha Hawkins worked at extracting the marrow while another team of doctors worked at keeping him alive.

The process was excruciatingly slow, as one long syringe after another was filled then placed in a receiving tray. Each stab of the needle weakened McCabe a little more than the last. Finally Hawkins pulled the last syringe from McCabe's hip.

"Okay, we got enough."

It was as if McCabe had stayed alive just long enough to hear those words. Almost instantly there was a high-pitched whine as the heart monitor flatlined.

"He's gone," said one of the doctors.

McCabe was dead. Frank Connor looked to Hawkins. ‘‘Is there time? Can we get it to Matt in time?’’

Samantha Hawkins nodded. ‘‘Oh yes,’’ she said with a weary smile. ‘‘He’ll make it. . . .’’